BIG TROUBLE IN A SMALL TOWN

BIG TROUBLE IN A SMALL TOWN

•

Jim Kennison

AVALON BOOKS
NEW YORK

Published by Thomas Bouregy & Co., Inc.
160 Madison Avenue, New York, NY 10016

Library of Congress Cataloging-in-Publication Data

Kennison, Jim.
Big trouble in a small town / Jim Kennison.
p. cm.
ISBN 978-0-8034-7761-2 (hardcover : acid-free paper)
I. Title.
PS3611.E6685B854 2010
813'.6—dc22
2009049910

PRINTED IN THE UNITED STATES OF AMERICA
ON ACID-FREE PAPER
BY HADDON CRAFTSMEN, BLOOMSBURG, PENNSYLVANIA

To Elletta, my wife and best friend,
who always keeps me focused.

Chapter One

If the Bartonville posse chasing Clemet Morgan had been real sheriffs, and if Morgan had broken the law, the story might have been different. But the badge-wearing thugs who were hot on his trail were the hired guns of land baron Jason Barton. Morgan had killed Barton's son, Chad. Barton's brand of justice would be quick and final if the posse overtook Morgan.

Chad Barton deserved killing. He was spoiled rotten and mean to everyone—especially women and old men who couldn't fight back. Morgan had watched the little bantam's shenanigans for most of the two days Morgan had spent in Bartonville. He didn't like what he saw, but considered it none of his concern. He would be out of town by morning.

Being the only son of the richest man in the territory,

Chad Barton had never worked a full day. His dandy clothes were always clean and the palms of his hands uncallused. The silver-plated .45s he wore in hand-tooled Spanish leather holsters matched perfectly with his silver buckles and large spurs. When he wasn't in the saloon he was sitting just outside its swinging doors, leaning back against the wall in a café chair, mouthing insults to all who walked by.

On the day Barton died he had reached out and grabbed the arm of a young woman as she and an old man walked in front of the saloon. The white-haired man took strong exception to Barton's advances and moved toward the two, yelling, "Keep your slimy hands off her!"

Barton's response was to draw his pistol and slam it into the side of the old man's head. Then, with a crazed look in his eyes, he turned on the girl. Trying to grab her, he ripped her dress.

Morgan watched as people on the street ran quickly into stores or rode away, leaving the girl and the old man to fend for themselves. Morgan's heart was pounding as he shouted at Barton, "Leave her alone. She's done nothing to you!"

Barton shoved the girl to the ground and spun around pointing his pistol in the direction of Morgan's voice. Without stopping to aim, Barton squeezed off a shot that grazed Morgan's shoulder before Morgan fast-drew his pistol and fired a slug into Barton's chest.

Chad Barton—town bully—lay dead in the dust.

Only then did people come back to the street, forming a circle around the boy's body as the girl cared for the battered old man struggling to regain his wits. She tore strips of cloth from her petticoat and bandaged his head wound.

Morgan held his pistol in a tight grip, not yet realizing all that had happened. He jerked away hard when he felt a hand on his shoulder. "Steady boy," a man said. "You best get that nick of yours taken care of, then get outta town as quick as you can."

"Why should I run?" Morgan asked. "He took the first shot and would've plugged me for sure if I hadn't got him first."

"You're right 'bout that, boy; but Jason Barton won't give a hoot in Hades if you fought fair. He'll only be lookin' to get revenge. You just killed his pride an' joy—his only son—an' the heir to his fortune."

"I'll tell my story to the sheriff the way it happened and if some of you folks back me up, it'll be okay."

The local gave Morgan a stern look.

"Ain't no one in this town gonna say the truth 'bout what went down here. We learned a long while back it's best just to go 'bout our business an' look the other way when a Barton's involved. Anyways, the sheriff's in ol' Jason's pocket an' on his payroll, so he won't be no help. You best skedaddle."

As quickly as they had come, the townspeople left again. Two men carried Barton's body into the saloon.

"Thank you," came a soft voice from the girl holding the old man's bleeding head in her lap. "Thank you for helping us. We don't even know that boy. We were just passing through town and planned to spend the night before going on. Why did he want to make trouble for us?"

"Just because you were handy, ma'am, would be my guess. I've been told I should be on my way real quick. I hope you'll be okay."

"I'm fine except for the cats in my stomach. I'll get help from someone to find a doctor for Grandpa."

Morgan knelt next to the old man. "Are you are going to be okay, old-timer?"

The man nodded slightly and faintly whispered, "Thanks."

"You're real welcome. Glad I could help." Morgan asked the girl for a strip of cloth to cover his bullet scratch then mounted his horse, waved good-bye to the two travelers sitting in the dusty street, and headed west at a gallop.

They were on the run and chase for three days. Morgan's only hope of getting away was to keep in front of the posse until they got tired or hungry and turned back to Bartonville. For sure he was tired and hungry, as was his horse.

On his last day of running, Morgan stayed in the saddle all night, putting distance between him and the posse. He saw the glow of the posse's campfire and knew his pursuers had stopped. He knew he couldn't. Reaching the bank of a stream just before dark, he slowed the horse's pace to a walk in the shallow water and followed the moon-lit current to throw the posse off track. When he left the stream and got back on solid ground, the gelding was exhausted.

The New Mexico sun was showing its first rays of morning as Morgan rode into the sleepy little town. Red Mountain wasn't much, but that was where he needed to be. Morgan was responding to a letter he'd received from a sheep rancher named Seth Ruddell, who wanted to hire Morgan to ply his skills as a private investigator and find who—or what—was responsible for the disappearance of a large number of his rams.

Thirty-year-old Clemet Morgan had cut his teeth learning the investigating business back East, working two years for Alan Pinkerton's agency. But in 1887, when the Pinkertons began hiring head-busters instead of thinkers, Morgan moved west to Pueblo and struck out on his own. He chose Pueblo because the population was growing and the amount of gold and silver that prospectors were finding in and around the Arkansas River made it necessary for mining companies to contract for security.

He had to make a few changes in adjusting to western living: Trading his bowler hat and three-piece suit for a Stetson and denim, and his small-frame Smith and Wesson revolver for a Colt .45. Fortunately, having grown up on a small cattle farm in Illinois, he was good around horses.

Providing security services for the mining companies was steady work but not too exciting. This began to change soon after he began advertising in the *Rocky Mountain*

News, with its large regional circulation. In fact, business picked up so fast that Morgan had taken on a partner to oversee the mining contracts, thus allowing Morgan to tackle more interesting projects. Morgan later learned it was one of his ads that had caught the eye of Ruddell.

Ruddell's letter told Morgan if he wanted the job to be in Red Mountain by the first of October; he was to tell no one why he was in town; and Ruddell would hire him as a ranch hand to cover Morgan's reason for being in the territory.

Red Mountain was still drowsy when Morgan arrived. He came across a building housing a blacksmith and livery stable and, to his surprise, found the door unlocked. He fed his horse a good helping of hay from the mow and put him into an empty stall between two beautiful Percherons. Then Morgan unwrapped his bedroll, stretched out in the hay, and fell asleep.

The rotund blacksmith roused Morgan from a deep sleep and stood over him with a shotgun pointed at his head.

"You better have a good reason why you're making yourself at home here in my barn," the man growled.

"Just drifting through looking for work," Morgan said, rubbing the sleep from his eyes. "Got to town real early this morning, so me and my horse were looking for a place to get a little shuteye. Be glad to pay you for the space."

"Nope, that won't need to happen. We don't get many strangers through here, but you look tame enough. Go on back to sleep, if you want, and I'll be getting to my chores. I'll start a pot of coffee brewing in the tack room. If you'd like some when it's perked, help yourself. I'm taking the wagon down to the feed store for some bags of grain. If you're still here when I get back, you can help me unload. We'll call that even for your bed."

"Fair enough. I'll be here. And maybe I can pick your brain a bit about places that might be hiring. I'd sure like to stay in one spot for a spell."

"Well, we can jaw on that—but it won't take long. I'll give it some thought while I'm getting the grain," the man said, leading the draft horses from the barn.

Morgan tried to get back to sleep but found it impossible. He got up, sopped his bandanna in the trough and scrubbed his beard stubble. He gingerly removed the blood-caked cotton strip from his shoulder wound and washed the scab. Digging into his saddlebag, he pulled out an almost-clean shirt and stuffed in the dirty one.

Try as he may, he couldn't shake the feeling of panicky fear that gripped his mind and body just minutes before being roused from his sleep. In his state of mental fatigue he dreamed the posse had caught up and was going to gun him down—or hang him from a barn rafter—without giving him a chance to reason with them.

By the time the liveryman got back an hour later, Morgan was better composed. Downing three cups of black coffee helped.

While they unloaded the wagon, the two made some talking time. The livery owner's name was Amos Porter.

He had moved to Red Mountain with his wife and daughter seventeen years before. His uncle had been the longtime owner of the livery and before his death—but knowing he was gravely ill—the uncle had sent for Porter. The timing was fortuitous in that Porter was trying to scratch a living on a small farm in Missouri and was more than ready to move. In addition to their daughter, the Porters had two sons, both born in Red Mountain. Porter quickly developed a strong interest in improving the community and, as a result, was elected mayor.

By the time they got around to the subject of available jobs, it was almost noon.

"Let's go on down the street to the house," Porter invited. "You can meet the missus, and we'll have a bite of lunch."

"That sounds good. I've been on the trail so long I'm not sure I'll be able to recognize anything that isn't jerky or hardtack."

Getting to the house, Porter excused himself to go inside and tell his wife they would be having company for lunch.

"Want to give her a chance to tidy up a bit if she thinks the house isn't presentable. Womenfolk can be funny that way."

Morgan smiled and nodded. There he stood, unshaven, smelly, in pants that were filthy and a shirt far from clean, and this gentle soul was concerned that their home might not be presentable. If this was an example of Red Mountain hospitality, Morgan thought, he could stay around for quite a spell. Inside the house, Morgan went directly to the washbasin and scrubbed his grimy hands with lye soap until they turned red.

Elsie Porter was taller than her husband and her slim build was in total contrast to his stoutness. The table—covered with bowls of cooked vegetables, a large platter of meat, and a basket of hot biscuits—looked like a holiday feast. A pitcher of buttermilk was within everyone's reach. The sideboard held a dish of fruit.

When Morgan expressed an interest in a family picture on the mantle, Elsie explained. Of the Porters' three children, daughter Lorna was in her early twenties and earned a small wage caring for a widower's two young girls. Lorna would ride to his house each weekday, freeing him to work his small ranch. The other two children were teenage boys, still in school. The picture showed Lorna to be very attractive.

Strolling back to the livery after lunch, the subject of finding work was finally broached.

"Well, Amos, how does it look? I'm not choosy about what I do, except I'd like to be out in the open."

"I've got to be honest with you—there isn't much work to be had around here this time of year. There's a lot of small crop farms close in toward town, but they're family–run and make do with the folks living under their roofs."

"I noticed those farms everywhere around the territory. Never been in New Mexico before, so I expected all deserts where nothing but cactus would grow."

"We have the Navajos to thank for working this land.

When they settled here a long time ago they figured out how to do lots of things with rivers and streams to irrigate their crops. They work real hard to harness water wherever they find it. And not just for themselves but for everyone hereabouts."

"I could maybe learn, but I don't think I'd make a very good farmer," Morgan confessed. "I've worked cattle."

"Most of the cattle being run on the larger spreads are already out on the open range for the winter, and the drovers who don't stay around the ranches to do maintenance find winter work in Mexico. Most of them come back up in the spring for the local roundups. You might want to think about doing that."

"Probably not. My rear end is so sore from being in the saddle, I don't think I'd last that many miles. What do you know about a man named Ruddell? I met a fellow on the trail who told me he thought they might be hiring."

"Hmmm. Well, that could be. Hadn't thought about what Seth might need for the winter. There's one thing you should know that might make a big difference in your decision: Seth Ruddell raises sheep. You ever worked with sheep?"

"No, but I'd never worked with cattle either until the first time, then I caught on real fast."

"Well, sheep aren't like cattle. Turn a cow loose and it'll find its own food and water and, for the most part, hold its own against coyotes and cougars. Sheep are like children. No, they're worse than children. Children have brains. Sheep need to be cared for night and day. They've got to be moved around from place to place to find grass or they'll eat everything they see—doesn't matter if it isn't good for them. You have to shove their noses into water or they die of thirst. They'll follow anything that moves. If a pack of coyotes stalk a herd of sheep, one is bound to run straight into the pack bleating, 'Here I am, eat me.' "

Morgan was laughing so hard at Porter's description of sheep he was unaware someone had entered the livery.

"Don't believe a word my father tells you about sheep. He likes his little joke; but he loves them when they're cooked."

"Lorna! What are you doing back in town so early?"

"One of the girls got sick and Al thought he needed to be with her, so I got to come home. Who's your scruffy friend?"

Lorna walked with long graceful strides toward the men. She wore black leather pants and a matching leather vest over a bright yellow blouse. She carried a riding quirt attached to her wrist by a short lanyard.

"His name's Clemet Morgan. He'll be staying around for a bit if he can find work. Clemet, this is my daughter, Lorna."

"Pleased to meet you," Morgan said as Lorna gave him a firm handshake. "When your mother told me you were looking after children, I expected to see you wearing a gingham dress."

"I keep a few dresses at Al's house and change when I

get there." Lorna laughed. "It's a lot more comfortable riding a horse in pants."

"You think Al could use Clemet out at the ranch Lorna?"

"I'm sure not. His three regular hands just took off to Mexico for the winter. The only one he's keeping on is his brother-in-law, Tommy. He hires extra help in the spring, though."

"Can't wait that long," Morgan replied. "I'm running short of cash, so I've got to hook up somewhere pretty quick."

"Clemet thinks maybe Seth Ruddell's hiring. You're a friend of his daughter. Has she said anything?"

"Not to me. Millie and her grandpa have been gone for almost two weeks. They drove their freight wagon to Farmington for a load of sheep dip. I don't think they're back yet; at least Millie hasn't been in town."

"Well, Clemet, it's too late for you to get out there today," Porter said. "Why don't you bed down here in the barn tonight and head out in the morning? Come by the house for supper and we'll loan you some pillows and heavy blankets. Lorna, tell your ma we'll be needing another place set at the table tonight."

"I'll do that right away. Since I'm home early, I'll bake something special for dessert."

Morgan watched with interest as Lorna left the barn.

What little sleep he managed came hard to Morgan. Although dinner with the Porters had been delicious and the conversation light and enjoyable, Morgan couldn't get his mind to slow down after returning to the livery for the night. His body still ached from the long hours of running ahead of the Bartonville posse and with every sound he imagined they were just outside the door.

Morgan's partner, Jamison Jakes, had made his living as a bounty hunter until just before his wife gave birth to their first child. He often talked of the fatigue and edginess he would feel during long days and sleepless nights of tracking bad guys through Colorado and Wyoming. Jakes was older and better suited than Morgan for the Ruddell assignment, and would have taken it, except he wanted to be close to home when his wife gave birth to their second child.

Jakes was a rugged individual who fought in the Civil War before drifting from place to place looking for some meaning to his life. He worked his way west as a scout for wagon trains. After that he put in time moving cattle from the Dakota Territory to Cheyenne. By his own count, before getting into the bounty hunting business eight years after the end of the war, Jakes had held eleven different jobs.

Becoming a professional bounty hunter gave his life a focus. Marrying a woman he met in Denver and becoming a family man gave his life meaning.

Morgan, up before the sun, found the coffee makings in the tack room. Halfway through his second cup, a voice called from the barn door, "Are you decent?" It was Lorna Porter.

"Sure am. Come on in. What gets you out so early?"

"On my way to look after Al's kids. His place is on the way to Ruddell's so I thought if we ride along together I can point you in the right direction."

It was a pleasant ride. The sun had finally peeked over the eastern horizon and its sparkling rays ware dancing on the early morning dew. The horses cantered smoothly side by side, the two riders seemingly lost in their own thoughts. Morgan spoke first.

"Have you been taking care of Al's kids for a long time?"

"About four months now. His wife's sickness was short before she died. At her funeral he asked me if I would care for the children until he found a new mother for them. I promised to do what I could, for as long as I could. But he hasn't made much progress in finding a new wife. Women in this part of the country are pretty scarce, especially single women."

"How about you? Seems like you fit the bill."

"Oh my, no." Lorna chuckled. "Al's an okay sort for the most part and a pretty good father. He's more strict with the kids than he should be, but I guess it's hard rearing children alone. The truth is, he's already married to that ranch. When I have a husband, I want to be able to see him once in a while. Besides, I plan to go to school and study to be a teacher. There's a new college opening in Silver City where my aunt and uncle live. I'll be moving there next fall."

"How big is Al's spread?"

"The Alawanda's not big as cattle ranches go. Just a few thousand acres. He breeds good stock and always gets top dollar. He wants to expand, but he's land-locked. Seth Ruddell's Rocking Ewe has him fenced off on three sides, and Al's south border runs into the mountains. But he knew what he was getting before he bought. The Ruddells had been in the territory raising sheep for ten years before Al and his new wife moved in."

"And Ruddell won't part with any of his spread?"

"No. In fact, it's something of an ongoing Mexican standoff. Each one wants the other's land, and they're constantly making offers and counter offers to see who'll give in first. They're friendly to each other and get along fine, but both are too stubborn to sell."

"You mentioned Al has a brother-in-law living with him."

"Yes. Tommy Hunt. His sister was Al's wife, Wanda. He moved down from Bartonville a couple years before Wanda died and he's been at Al's ranch ever since."

"What did Wanda die from?"

"No one knows for sure. She was in a lot of pain for quite a while. Her older sister died of something similar a few years before."

"So what's your read on Tommy?"

"He's an odd duck. Pretty quiet and standoffish for the most part, except when it comes to Millie Ruddell. He has a bad case of lovesickness over Millie that gets pretty embarrassing at times."

"How so?"

"The way he follows her around, looking like a sick calf, when they're in town at the same time. He'll go into stores where she's shopping and try to pay for what she's buying. When she won't allow that, he'll make a big deal out of carrying her purchases to the wagon. Once he tried to kiss her in front of everyone at a church picnic, and Al sent Tommy home. He hasn't been so bad lately, but I think Millie's afraid of him."

"That's too bad. Sounds like Cupid's arrow hit him real good."

"That's a nice way of putting it." Lorna laughed.

"From what I've seen, Red Mountain seems like a real nice spot. Do you like it here?"

"I love it. The people are wonderful. We're one big family, all spread out. When someone needs help, everyone pitches in. Like when it's shearing time at the Ruddell place, dozens of neighbors—including Al Robertson—will show up to help. And they don't expect pay because they know when their crops come in old Seth will be right alongside them, helping bring in the harvest, and working with Al at branding time."

Reaching a crossroad, the girl turned south and told Morgan to keep going for another five miles to find the Rocking Ewe. Morgan watched Lorna ride off at a gallop until she was out of sight.

It was a half-hour before Morgan saw any sign of life, and that was at a distance. He had followed a barbed wire fence line for some time before knowing its purpose. On the sides of numerous rolling hills, he made out the forms of hundreds of sheep leisurely grazing inside another large area, also surrounded by barbed wire. Two men on horseback at the edge of the compound, along with three dogs in among the flock, were in control. Morgan found a gate in the roadside fence and cantered toward the men. When he was fifty yards away, the man closest to Morgan took his rifle from its scabbard.

"That's close enough, hombre!" the man yelled. "Stop right there!"

"Hey, I'm friendly," Morgan shouted back, holding both arms high to show the man he wasn't going to cause trouble.

The man rode toward him. "What do you want?"

"Just a fella out of work, trying to find some. Are you part of the Ruddell crew? I hear he might be taking on some more hands."

"Don't know nothin' 'bout that. We been out here rotatin' these sheep fer a month or more. Don't see the old man much; could be he's lookin' to hire. Lord knows, we could use extra help. He's got more'n twenty flocks like this one strung out across his land."

"How do I find him?"

"Keep goin' down that road you was on, an' at the end of it you'll find his house. If he is hirin', tell him Harry Samuels, that's me, an' my pardner, Swift Eagle, that's him over there, would like first dibs on you."

"Okay, Harry, I'll sure do that. Name's Clemet Morgan. Hope to see you again."

"Same here. Sorry I pulled my fire stick, but we've

been havin' some real trouble. We been told to challenge every stranger we see."

"What kind of trouble?"

"Don't rightly know for sure. The old man's pretty tightlipped. But he's a straight shooter an' if he signs you on he'll let you know what he thinks you need to know."

"Fair enough. Thanks for the warning."

Morgan rode at an easy trot and tried to make sense of Harry Samuels' comments. Interesting that Samuels knew Ruddell was having a hard time but didn't know what was causing it. In his letter, Ruddell told Morgan the big problem was the systematic disappearance of Ruddell's rams. Maybe Ruddell was suspicious of everyone, even his own crew. On the other hand, was Ruddell trying to keep the problem as close to home as he could? Morgan was eager to meet Ruddell and get some answers.

By mid-afternoon Morgan found the ranch house. It was large and could be seen from quite a distance. Tall cottonwoods protected the house on the west and south sides and a large windmill loomed in the rear. A number of outbuildings dotted the landscape, a hundred yards or more from the house. Most prominent were two main barns and what appeared to be a sheep-dip shelter. There was no life around the house and the barnyard looked deserted.

Remembering Samuels' warning that all strangers would be challenged, Morgan reined in his gelding, stood as tall as he could in the stirrups and shouted, "Hello, the house!" After two more shouts, the front door opened slowly and a rifle barrel poked out.

"Who are you, and what do you want?" It was a woman's voice.

"My name is Clemet Morgan. I'm here to see Seth Ruddell."

The door closed and Morgan heard the click of a lock. In a few minutes, the door was unlocked, and a young woman stepped out onto the porch.

"You can come in. Grandpa said he's been expecting you. Sorry about the unfriendly welcome."

"No problem ma'am. It pays to be careful."

Morgan dismounted and wrapped the gelding's reins around the hitching post. As he neared the porch, the girl let out a gasp. "It's you! You're the man who helped us in Bartonville!"

The mention of the town stopped Morgan in his tracks. He stood in disbelief, looking at the teary-eyed girl standing in front of him.

"Millie? Are you Millie Ruddell?"

"Yes. And you're the one who saved Grandpa's life when you shot that horrible boy. We thought we'd never see you again, to tell you how thankful we are for your help."

Ruddell appeared at the door, walking with the help of crutches. He was even more surprised than his granddaughter at the sight of Morgan.

"My word, son. I had no idea! We thought you'd be in Mexico by now."

Chapter Two

Before talking in detail about the reason Seth Ruddell had sent for Clemet Morgan, Ruddell first wanted to fill him in on what happened after Morgan made his hurried exit from Bartonville.

In less than two hours word reached Jason Barton that his son was dead and Barton, with a dozen of his men, assembled in town to deal with the murderer. The doctor who treated Ruddell made him take a room in the hotel so he could rest and recuperate from his beating. Thinking of what might have happened, Millie was so shaken by the events of the afternoon that she could do little more than sit next to the bed, watching her grandpa—thankful he was still alive.

Barton wasted no time ordering the sheriff to deputize Barton's gang and hit the trail to catch his son's killer.

Barton stayed behind in the empty saloon to be alone with his dead son, and the townsfolk on the street could hear his sorrowful mourning. After an hour or so, the undertaker entered the saloon with three helpers, who draped Chad Barton's body with a velvet cloth and moved the boy to the funeral home.

Soon after, there was a knock on Seth's and Millie's hotel door. It was Jason Barton, holding a bottle of whiskey in one hand and a glass in the other. It was important for him to meet the people his son died protecting. Downing shot after shot of whiskey, he related what witnesses to the killing told him had happened: A stranger rode into town, got liquored up and tried to kiss Millie on the street, in broad daylight. While Seth tried to keep the attacker away from Millie, the stranger beat the old man with his pistol. Leaping to their defense, Chad Barton was gunned down in cold blood. Chad was a hero.

Morgan could do little more than slowly shake his head as the story unfolded.

"I was about to set Barton straight," Ruddell said, "but Millie shushed me up real quick. I guess, in hindsight, keeping quiet was the best thing to do."

"Nothing would have been gained by telling Barton the truth," Millie explained. "He was told what he needed to hear. If we had gone against the story, he would have called us liars, and made our lives even more miserable. I just wanted to get out of that wretched place and get Grandpa home. The doctor said to not move Grandpa for at least two days, but we left early the next morning.

Along with getting his head bashed in, Grandpa cracked a bone in his leg when he fell."

"Can't blame you for not going up against Barton," Morgan said. "Maybe all this will settle down after a while and folks will forget about it."

"That's not likely," Ruddell responded. "Old man Barton's in a world of grief. He's put out a big reward for anyone who brings in the killer. On the good side, everything happened so fast when you shot Chad, nobody really has a good recollection of what you look like. Some say you're tall and others say you're short; some have you young while others swear you got gray hair. I'd say, so long as you don't go anywhere near Bartonville, you'll be okay."

"That'll be the last place in creation I'll ever go near," Morgan stated firmly. "The very last place."

Later, over coffee, Ruddell spelled out the problem that prompted his sending for Morgan. Ruddell had been raising sheep for a dozen years. He was into cattle for a long time before that; but when more beef was being grown than there was a good market for, he changed to sheep. Sheep were a lot harder, but Ruddell was the only commercial wool and mutton provider in the entire region. The Navajos had herds larger than Ruddell's, but they used their animals only to feed and clothe their tribe and weren't interested in venturing beyond that.

Ruddell had done very well, expanding his enterprise as far as he cared to. Then something strange and worrisome began to happen: Ruddell noticed a number of his mature rams went missing. He kept a tight yearly inventory on the rams so the very old could be culled, making room for younger ones. During the first year of depletion, seventeen mature rams had disappeared. In the year just past, he had lost thirty. One good lamb ram can impregnate twenty-five ewes during a breeding season and a mature ram, thirty-five. The rams are kept apart from the ewes except for a few weeks in late fall when they're turned loose in the folds to breed with the ewes. Once the work is done they're returned to their own holding areas until needed again. Ruddell had three separate ram flocks spread throughout his ranch.

These two losses combined could account for as many as fourteen hundred ewes not being bred. It was obvious to Ruddell that someone was trying to sabotage his operation. But who and why? It would be Morgan's job to find the answers.

Morgan, Ruddell and Millie sat up late talking about how to start the process. It was important for Morgan to be seen as a hired ranch hand so no one would suspect he was a detective or that Ruddell had sent for him. Ruddell told Millie to keep Morgan's real identity under her bonnet.

Finally, a plan emerged. Ruddell had never used a manager to look after the workings of his spread. He took great pride and satisfaction in being a hands-on owner. Now things were different. The injuries Ruddell sustained from the Chad Barton beating left him unable to ride, and he needed crutches to walk. In assuming the role of ranch manager, Morgan would have full run of the spread with the ability to be wherever he felt he should at any time. No questions asked. He would also have responsibility for driving the wagon into Red Mountain each Saturday to pick up supplies for the following week. This would allow him to meet a number people, expanding the possibility of getting useful information.

The ranch hands needed to know they had a new boss. Throughout the more than five-thousand acres making up the Rocking Ewe, Ruddell had built forty-two very large folds. He then divided the flocks, using twenty-one separate folds at any given time. Each of the folds had a small shack with two beds and a cook stove, and a privy just outside the door. Having twice as many folds as needed at one time allowed the rotation of the sheep into new stands of grass. Each fold had a water supply coming from large hand-dug wells feeding into watering holes. When grass was scarce, hay would be delivered from the ample supply that filled the large barns near the ranch house. Two shepherds and three dogs tended each flock and every Sunday one man from each fold came to the ranch house to make a weekly report and pick up supplies. At Sunday's meeting, Morgan would be introduced and his job responsibilities discussed. Those present at the meeting would take the word back to their partners.

Becoming known in Red Mountain was also an important part of the equation. It was decided that Morgan and Millie would drive into town the next day so Millie could introduce Morgan to merchants who carried accounts for Seth Ruddell's supplies.

This was a good decision, Morgan told himself during what was left of a restless night. His lodging was a room in the corner of the bigger barn, making it easy to have the horses hitched up an hour before the breakfast bell clanged.

The trip into town took more than two hours each way, giving Morgan and Millie a chance to get acquainted. Morgan's first question was, "How did you end up here in the middle of nowhere, living with your grandpa?"

Millie didn't answer immediately, as she pondered the question.

"I was moving here from Iowa with my parents. Grandpa sent for my dad, hoping he'd come out. Since our farm went through two bad years of growing corn, the time seemed right to make a move. The folks sold everything except some of the furniture, and we started for here in the early spring. This was almost fifteen years ago, just before my third birthday."

"Where are your folks now?"

"They're dead. They both drowned when we tried to ford a river. The place Pa picked to cross was too deep and swift. I don't remember any of what happened. I only know what I've been told by Grandpa, from what he was able to figure out."

"How is it you didn't drown?"

"Grandpa says I was in my wooden cradle, sleeping he supposes. He doesn't know how far I drifted with the current before the bed caught in a logjam. Then, he says a Navajo hunter heard me crying and was able to pull me to the bank. The man, Swift Eagle, now works for Grandpa."

"I met him! He was with another hand named Harry Samuels."

"That's right. Harry and Swift Eagle have been partners for years."

"Sure was lucky for you that Swift Eagle knew who you were, so he could get you to your grandpa."

"In fact, Swift Eagle had no idea who I was. He took me to his village and his mother looked after me in their hogan like I was her own child. But, for my sake, she wanted to find my family. The only clue was my first name carved in the foot of the cradle. Swift Eagle took that piece of wood and carried it with him everywhere he went. Whenever he saw white people, he would show them the name. He spoke only the Navajo language then, so showing my name carved on that piece of wood was all he could do."

"How did he finally find your grandpa?"

"As the story goes, after many weeks of looking, Swift Eagle's mother sent him into Red Mountain and told him to not come home until he found out who I was. Since the Navajos used the reservation trading post for all their supplies, he had never been to a white man's town. Swift Eagle would sit in front of the general store from sunup to sunset, holding that piece of wood. At night, he would disappear into the darkness, but every morning he'd be back. Kids teased him about being a man with a woman's name, and the grownups thought he was touched in the head.

"Then, after more than a week, a man came up to Swift Eagle and tried to have a conversation. He'd heard there was an Indian with a piece of wood with a name on it. That man was Grandpa. He was so excited! Using sign language, and some sounds between the two men, Grandpa knew I was alive. The two rode hard to Swift Eagle's hogan, and there I was.

"The next evening, they had a farewell feast for me. I remember the drumming and dancing. Every member of the village passed by where I was sitting on Grandpa's lap and touched my head. The following morning, Swift Eagle rigged a traveling sled for Grandpa's horse and he brought me home. I still go visit Swift Eagle's mother when I can."

"That's quite a story. How is it that Swift Eagle works for your grandpa?"

"I suppose part of it was Grandpa's way of saying thanks. Grandpa hired Swift Eagle and three other Navajo men to help work his spread. All these men are steady and reliable; they're real good hands."

The two drove in silence for some time, caught up in the surrounding beauty. The sun was brilliant in midmorning splendor. Small dust devils swirled alongside the wagon. A hawk circled leisurely above the trail, casting its large shadow over the wagon and the two travelers, ready to swoop down quickly to snatch a hapless cottontail or prairie dog in its mighty talons. Butcherbirds darted in and out of their homes, built among the spines of prickly pear cactus. Small animals scurried through the brush, talking to each other with squeaks and chirps and throaty growls. The sound of the wagon flushed a covey of quail, and a pair of coyotes moved quietly away from the scent of humans.

Approaching the crossroad where Lorna Porter had said good-bye to Morgan the day before, they saw a man sitting astride his horse, rolling a cigarette. He seemed surprised when the two got close enough to be recognized.

"Hey, Millie!" the man shouted. "Why you headed to town today? This ain't Saturday."

"Hi, Tommy. Grandpa just hired a new manager. I'm taking him into town to show him around. What are you doing out this way so early?"

"Just lookin' for stray calves. Al sends me out sometimes, just to be sendin' me out. He knows I ain't gonna find none, but he still has me go. If you ask me, I think it's so he can be alone with that Lorna woman."

Morgan felt a twinge of jealousy at the mention of Lorna's name, thinking what Tommy was saying might be true.

"Anyway," Millie continued, "this is Clemet Morgan and he'll be around for quite some time—at least until Grandpa's back on his feet."

"Is your grandpa ailin'?"

"He had a bad accident in Bartonville on our way

home from Farmington last week. He has a cracked leg and some sore ribs. He'll be laid up for a spell."

"So, Morgan," Hunt said, showing little concern for Ruddell's health, "you ain't from 'round here. Where'd you come from an' what brings you to these parts?"

"I'm from up north," Morgan replied curtly. "I came down here looking for work. Seth needed help, so I hired on."

"Where from up north? An' why'd you come this direction lookin' for work?"

"Just wanted a change, if it's any of your business," Morgan replied, thinking of Lorna and what she might be doing back at Robertson's ranch.

"What if I make it my business?" Hunt shot back, pushing himself up as tall as possible in his stirrups.

"Don't go down that road, boy."

"I'm not a boy! Come down off that wagon an' I'll prove it."

Morgan started to get up from the wagon seat but thought better of it. Millie had seen more than her share of violence the past few days.

"Stop it! Both of you just stop it right now! Quit acting like children! Tommy, go on to wherever you were headed. We have to get into town; so be on your way."

"Okay, Millie. I'll do it for you." Then he looked menacingly at Morgan and delivered a parting shot. "We'll cross trails again sometime—when you ain't got a woman 'round to protect you."

"I look forward to that," Morgan replied calmly. "I surely do."

Hunt whooped loudly and reared his horse before galloping away.

The wagon team was encouraged to move a bit faster to make up for the time lost during the encounter with Hunt. Millie looked straight ahead, her jaw set and her eyes flashing.

"He's a snot-nose little brat," Morgan fumed.

"And I thought for a minute you were going to be a snot-nose big brat," Millie shot back. "What is it about you men that you feel the need to go at each others' throats? I can understand what Tommy was doing. It's no secret he's sweet on me. He was trying to impress me by putting a burr under your saddle. But why did you almost take his bait?"

"Sorry, Millie. The kid rubbed me the wrong way with the first words out of his mouth. Do you think there's any truth to what he was saying about Robertson and Lorna Porter?"

"Do you know Lorna?"

"I met her in Red Mountain and got to know her family some. She and I rode out this way yesterday morning. We had a real good talk. I guess you could say I know her a little."

"So that's it," Millie sighed. "Another man thing. She looks good to you and can hold her own in a conversation so you're already building a fire to get your branding iron hot."

Chapter Three

Clemet Morgan and Millie returned from Red Mountain to the Rocking Ewe just before dark. While Morgan unloaded the wagon in the barn, Millie prepared dinner. For the most part it had been a good day. Millie introduced Morgan around town to the merchants where Seth Ruddell had credit and bought supplies for the next week.

After a quick lunch at the Good Grub Café, Millie shopped for a new dress to replace the one that had been ripped by Chad Barton. This gave Morgan time to swing by the livery stable and chat with Amos Porter. Porter was pleased to hear that Ruddell had not only hired Morgan, but made him the boss.

"Pays to be in the right place when the time's right, that's for sure," Morgan responded. As much as he wanted to ask Amos questions about Lorna, he decided enough was enough for one day and, besides, he would be coming into Red Mountain every Saturday. He would have lots of chances to see her. He asked Porter to carry a "hello" and another thanks for the family's hospitality.

Morgan was in the saddle at daybreak wanting to get a feel for the expanse of the Rocking Ewe before meeting the hands at Sunday's meeting. Ruddell had drawn a rough map, showing monuments that approximated the corners of the spread. Circles and numbers marked the current sheepfolds. The two agreed Morgan should keep his distance until the shepherds got to know him by sight, thus preventing his being shot as an intruder.

Ruddell's crew were all good men who wouldn't go out of their way looking for trouble. It helped to hear most were fiercely loyal to the old man. Ruddell treated them fairly, paid good wages, and could be counted on to keep the herd numbers high enough to ensure they always had jobs. But this was now a serious concern to Ruddell. If Morgan couldn't find the underlying cause of what was happening to the rams, the loss of jobs would follow the loss of sheep.

In the short time Morgan had known Ruddell, he was learning to respect and admire the man. Ruddell had carved a small empire out of this hard land. He was raising Millie by himself and made sure she got a good education. Clearly another measure of the man showed through—he hadn't let discouragement get the best of him after Barton broke his bones.

Morgan reflected on his only reason for coming to Red Mountain, which had been to earn the fee Ruddell promised to pay him for his detective work. Now, more than anything else, he wanted to make sure this good man stayed in business.

Riding through the vastness of the Rocking Ewe, Morgan pondered the situation. Nothing made sense. If someone wanted to hurt Ruddell's operation in a big way, why not just ride roughshod through all the flocks and shoot the sheep? The mystery of the disappearing rams had to be solved or the result would be the same—Ruddell would be shut down.

It was after dark when Morgan returned to the ranch house, having seen enough of the spread to get a fix on the basic logistics. It was rich and fertile land with sufficient streams running from the mountains to keep grass growing and available. A great place to raise sheep.

A lamp was burning in the living room, so Morgan unsaddled his horse, brushed it some to get rid of the dust, put it in a stall and headed for the house to share his first impression of the Rocking Ewe.

He knocked lightly at the front door and looked inside the room through the window. Deciding that Ruddell and Millie had gone to bed leaving the lamp still lit, he turned to leave the porch. Hearing hoofbeats galloping away from the back of the house stopped him cold in his tracks. He followed the sound as quickly as he could in the dark, revolver in hand, knowing something was happening that shouldn't be.

Morgan returned to the porch, and this time he shouted, "Seth, this is Morgan! Are you all right? Millie, are you in the house?"

"Yes, we're both here. I'll unlock the door."

Millie stood shaking in the doorway, holding a rifle tightly, her face tense. When she saw Morgan, she dropped the rifle and slumped to the floor. Morgan rushed to help her up and, once standing, she clung tightly to his shoulders and buried her face in his chest. She began sobbing uncontrollably.

"What is it, Millie? What's going on?"

"Someone was here making strange noises, like an animal in pain. Then howling like a coyote, and laughing like a crazy man. We heard rocks hitting the roof. It would be quiet for a couple of minutes and then he would start all over again. I shouted for him to stop, to go away and leave us alone, but he laughed even louder. Grandpa tried to get out of bed after the first noises started, but he fell and couldn't get up. He's really hurting. A few minutes before you got here, the man heaved a stick of firewood and smashed the kitchen window.

"I wanted to shoot out through the broken window, hoping I'd hit him; but I was too terrified to pull the trigger."

"Do you have any idea who it could be?"

"No! And that makes it even scarier. If we knew someone had it in for us, we might be able to understand what caused this. Grandpa gets along with everyone. Sure, he can drive a hard bargain when it comes to buying or selling, but people expect that of him. They know he's honest and fair."

"Well, give it some thought. If you come up with anything, any detail, no matter how small, let me know right away.

"Let's go check on Seth and then you get to bed. I'll sleep here on the sofa tonight in case that peckerwood decides to come back."

Morgan went to the barn, fed his horse, and got some blankets before returning to the house. All the while he was trying to sort out what just happened to Ruddell and Millie. Could this bizarre evening have a connection to the missing rams?

By mid-morning the ranch hands started drifting in for the Sunday report meeting. Clemet Morgan had awakened early to the smell and sound of perking coffee. Millie always had coffee and sweet cakes ready when the men arrived. This assured they would show up on time, before all the cakes were eaten. When the meetings started, Millie would begin cooking dinner. The men appreciated Millie's cooking and she liked giving them a good meal before they headed back to their posts on the range.

Before the men arrived, Morgan and Ruddell had a

chance to talk about the night before. Ruddell was as clueless as Millie as to who might have been howling outside the house. The guesses ranged from someone bent on scaring them for a purpose, to a drunk looking for some fun. Either way it was very weird behavior—with no apparent reason.

Morgan was introduced to the men as they arrived. He made careful note of anything unusual that might indicate if one of these guys could have been the crazy night visitor. Nervous movements? Shifty eyes? Not able to relax?

With all the men seated and ready to start the meeting, Morgan ruled out everyone in the room except a man named Lester Hobson. Hobson looked at the floor most of the time, not making eye contact with anyone. While the others swapped jokes and lies, Hobson was totally quiet, never smiling.

Ruddell did a good job explaining to the men about Morgan and why he needed Morgan to be his legs and eyes until Ruddell could get up and around. Seeing Ruddell in his banged-up condition and hobbling slowly on crutches was all the convincing they needed. No mention was made of the strange happenings of the night before.

Only when Ruddell asked the group if they had any questions did Hobson speak.

"I don't cotton to a feller none a' us knows comin' in here an' runnin' things. Some a' us been with you from the start, Seth, an' I fer one think one a' us ought a' git the chance a' bein' ramrod."

"Sorry you feel that way, Lester," Ruddell replied. "But running this spread is a big job, and it needs someone with a head for business; someone who can deal with the merchants in Red Mountain, and who can find the best buyers for the wool and mutton."

"You sayin' none a' us is smart enough to go to town?" Hobson's voice had an edge.

"No, Lester, that's not what I'm saying at all. You men are the best I've ever known for doing the job you're hired to do. Morgan couldn't do your jobs half as good as you do them. You're needed to keep doing what you do best. But we've all got to work together to make a go of this place."

"Well, if I'm as good as you say I am, maybe I'm too good to stay 'round. Maybe it's time I move on. I worked cows long 'fore I come to be a part a' your operation. Could be I'll just go on down to Mexico an' hook up with a' outfit that treats its crew like they was men."

"Then you go!" It was the booming voice of Swift Eagle. "No one treat us better than Seth. When we sick, he work for us 'til we be well. After we shear, he give us time to go home with family, and still pay us. We keep work when times be bad. Where you find better place?"

A loud chorus of "amen" came from the other men. Hobson went to the front porch and rolled a cigarette. Ruddell hobbled after him.

"Dagnabit, Lester, what in thunder's going on with you?"

"They ain't nothin' goin' on. Just can't figure how

some stranger can come ridin' in here an' in a week be runnin' the dadburn show. They's gotta be somethin' you ain't tellin'."

"You know all you need to know, Lester. Let it go at that." Ruddell was beginning to sound angry. "I don't want you to leave, but if that's what you feel you need to do, then all I'm asking is that you stay on until I can find someone to fill in. You owe me that much. Come inside and have some dinner before it gets cold."

"Okay, Seth," Hobson said, crushing the partly smoked cigarette on the porch banister and putting the butt in his shirt pocket. "I'll stick 'round fer a while. But I'm gonna keep a real sharp eye on that Morgan feller."

Chapter Four

Clemet Morgan waited until Tuesday before heading out to visit the twenty-one working folds, giving the men who attended Sunday's meeting the chance to explain to their partners what was going on. His goal was to get to as many folds as possible each day, visiting them all in the three days he had set aside; but he wasn't concerned if that didn't happen.

Although Morgan would be going to Red Mountain for supplies on Saturday, he decided to head in on Monday as well. He was bothered about Ruddell and Millie being alone for the three nights he would be out on the range, but Ruddell assured him he could handle anything that might come up, now that he knew what to expect. He would sleep during the day—staying awake at night—rifle at the ready.

While Morgan admired Ruddell's grit, he still worried

Millie might have a problem dealing with another visit from a crazy man. After a great deal of persuasion Millie agreed to go with Morgan into Red Mountain and spend the week with the Porters. They would go into town on horseback and Morgan would bring her home on Saturday.

Reaching Red Mountain a little after noon, Morgan took Millie directly to the livery stable, told Amos Porter what had happened at the ranch, and explained the need for Millie to stay with the Porters for a few days.

"That'll be just fine," Porter said through a broad grin. "Lorna will really enjoy spending time with a girl near her own age for a change."

The mention of Lorna's name sent a quick but pleasant tingling up Morgan's spine. Porter put the OUT TO LUNCH sign on the livery door so he could take Millie to the house.

"Is Lorna home?"

This was the question Morgan was hoping Millie would ask. He was disappointed with the answer.

"No, like most days, she's out caring for Al's children. But she has shorter hours now, so she'll be along by supper time. Since you've got your horse, Millie, you might want to go along with her tomorrow. The two of you can visit more while she's looking after the young'uns."

Morgan was invited to go along to Porter's house before heading back to the Rocking Ewe. He declined the invitation, saying it was getting late.

In truth, he wanted to pay the sheriff a visit.

Morgan had ridden past the small building with a hand-painted sign reading TOWN SHERIFF & JAIL, and figured filling the sheriff in as to who he was and why he was living at the Rocking Ewe would be good politics. But how much should he tell? The whole story, starting with his letter from Seth Ruddell asking for help? The trouble with the disappearing rams? And what about his killing the boy in Bartonville? That was, after all, the first time Morgan met Ruddell, and would serve to explain Ruddell's 'accident' that put him out of commission.

Reaching the sheriff's office, Morgan read a weathered sign hanging from a nail stating the sheriff could be found at the general store. Morgan had been in the store with Millie when they visited the week before and was impressed with the extent of inventory. Millie introduced him to the wife of the store's owner who helped him find everything on his list of needs for the Rocking Ewe.

As he entered the store, the woman looked up from the book she was reading and greeted him with a broad smile.

"Why, I do declare," she said cheerfully, "if it isn't Mr. Morgan. What brings you back so soon? We didn't expect to see you until Saturday. Did you forget something you couldn't do without?"

"No, ma'am. Millie wanted to come into town to spend a few days visiting with Lorna Porter, so I came along for the ride. I'll be in on Saturday with the wagon. I stopped by the sheriff's office to make his acquaintance and found a note on the door that he'd be at the store. Guess I missed him."

"Oh, gracious no. He's still here. He's out back helping

the freight man unload some heavy things. You wait while I let him know you're looking for him. He'll be right in."

True to her word, in less than a minute the woman was back in the store with a man following close behind.

"Harold, this is Clemet Morgan. He's the new hire out to Seth Ruddell's place. He'll be filling Seth's boots until Seth gets spry again, so we'll be seeing quite a bit of him."

"Pleased to meet you, Clemet. I'm Harold Gainer. My wife Nell and I own this business. Been here more years than I care to remember." There was a note of pride in Harold's voice.

"You got a real nice place. Don't ever remember a store in a town this size that carried so much merchandise."

"We're the only general store anywhere around, and folks appreciate they don't have to go all the way to Bartonville to get most of what they need. I also run the telegraph station from a room in the back. We're too far off the beaten path to get much overland mail; if we're lucky it'll come and go two or three times a month. When it does come, we're the post office too. There's no saloon in town, so we keep some bottled whiskey here under the counter for those who want to take it home."

"Seems like you're able to take care of just about everybody. But the main reason I stopped by was to have a talk with the sheriff; is he still out back?"

"No, sir, he's standing right here," Harold said with a broad grin, reaching into his apron pocket. He pulled out a badge and pinned it to the apron's bib.

"Folks hereabout thought we should have some law in the area, so the town council asked me to be the sheriff. No one's sure about how much territory should be considered as Red Mountain, so I set my limit to wherever I can get within a half-day's ride. Past that, people are on their own."

"Enough of that," Nell said. "Clemet's looking for the sheriff and now he's found you. Hush and see what he wants."

"There were some pretty bad things going on at Ruddell's last night," Morgan said. "Some crazy galoot was making animal sounds and howling like a coyote. Then he threw rocks on the roof to make a racket. The last thing he did, before I came riding in and scared him off, was to chuck a piece of firewood through the kitchen window glass."

"Oh, merciful heavens!" Nell said, almost in a shout. "That's terrible! Who would do such a horrible thing?"

"Somebody who's got it in for Seth would be my guess," the sheriff responded. "Did you get any look at him at all? Could you see what kind of horse he was riding?"

"No, nothing. It was after dark. I'd put away my horse before I heard about the commotion. Millie was really shook up. Just thought you should know, Sheriff, in case you hear of anything going on; or if I bring someone into town draped over his saddle."

"Well, a skunk like that is sure fair game," the sheriff replied. "If you catch him alive bring him in and I'll toss the sorry piece of trash in the lockup."

"Thanks, Harold. If he's lucky enough to be alive when I'm through with him, I'll do just that."

Riding back to the Rocking Ewe, Morgan reassessed the situation. Harold Gainer was the only law in the region but because he was a store clerk first and a sheriff second, Harold couldn't be much help, except to provide a jail cell. Morgan felt he had shared all he should with the Gainers. No need for them to hear the real reason Morgan was in the area and, for sure, the sheriff didn't need to know about the death of Chad Barton.

Morgan slowed his horse's pace to almost a walk. With some good fortune, maybe he'd pass Lorna Porter on her way home from Robertson's ranch. When he hadn't seen her by the time he reached the crossroad where they parted company a few days before, he picked up speed to a trot and then a full gallop. Maybe Lorna took another route home.

In any event, Ruddell would be wondering, or even worrying about the events of the day. Certainly, Morgan had his own concerns regarding the welfare of Seth Ruddell. The more Morgan heard people speak to the kind of man Seth was, the more Morgan liked him.

From a distance, Morgan saw smoke rising from the ranch house chimney and knew a hot supper was waiting. Even on crutches, Ruddell was a good host.

Chapter Five

At first light Clemet Morgan was in the saddle to make the rounds of the sheepfolds. After getting back to the ranch house in the evening, he nailed boards over the kitchen window hole. He and Ruddell talked until past dark, devising a strategy for solving the disappearing rams mystery.

Morgan would go to every fold, interview the hands to get as much information as he could, and explain what was going on. It was time they knew about the problem Ruddell was facing. However, no need yet to tell the men Morgan was a private detective, or that Ruddell had sent for him. This would come about in due course.

Morgan decided to skip the fold where Swift Eagle and Harry Samuels worked. He'd met Samuels on his way to Ruddell's and Swift Eagle had attended Sunday's meeting. Morgan was impressed with both men. They were not on his mental list of suspects.

The man he wanted to see first and foremost was Lester Hobson, the only person at Sunday's meeting who spoke out against Morgan being made ramrod. If there was going to be bad blood between the two, they may as well find out now rather than later.

Morgan understood why Hobson was upset for not being picked by Ruddell to be ranch manager; but there was something more about Hobson that didn't quite fit with the rest of the crew. For one thing, Hobson seemed disinterested in everything discussed at the meeting except Morgan's hiring. His thoughts were somewhere else—not in the meeting room. Morgan was also curious as to why Swift Eagle reacted as he did to Hobson's threat to quit and move on. Had these two butted heads before? If so, why and when? Morgan needed answers to those questions to see if they had any bearing on the case.

Hobson and his partner, a man named Jed Nooley, were working in an area farthest from the ranch house. He reasoned this would also be his most difficult session. Because of the tension the men were feeling with their orders to challenge all strangers riding through, Morgan told the men at the meeting when he approached a fold he would tie a white flag to his rifle and hold it high in the air, signaling he was a friend.

If nothing else, he hoped Hobson had paid enough attention during the meeting to hear that announcement.

Looking at the map Ruddell had drawn of the folds,

Morgan figured he could get to no more than three on this day; but they were the ones that were farthest apart. Not too far from the third was a vacant crew shack where he would spend the night.

He planned to spend time the following day at both ram folds, the scenes of the disappearances. Ruddell had a long-standing practice of rotating the crew teams, so that no one team had to spend more than a week at a time with the rams. Because of the rams' rowdiness, and their penchant for fighting, they needed to be more closely tended than the ewes or the lambs. Ruddell figured the rams went missing during the crew shift.

Well before reaching the fold being worked by Hobson and Nooley, Morgan tied the white flag, made from one of Millie's pillowcases, to the barrel of his Winchester and held it high in the air. When the flock came into view he began waving the flag back and forth in a broad sweeping motion, making sure it would be seen. Within minutes, dust was kicked up by someone riding hard from the area of the fold, and then slowed as the two riders got closer to each other. It was Lester Hobson.

"My pardner's been shot!" Hobson yelled. "He's been shot, an' he's dead!"

"Hold on, Hobson. Simmer down. How did it happen? When did it happen?"

"Last night. We was fixin' to hit the hay when the dogs started barkin' like crazy an' Nooley went to check, an' I heard a shot an' Nooley yelled, an' them dang dogs wouldn't shut their yappin'. Then I hear a horse goin' outta here like they was a fire in his tail, an' Nooley come back through the door holdin' his gut. He just dropped dead on the floor.

"I covered him over with a blanket an' at first light this mornin' I got him in the ground."

"Where did you bury him?"

"Right out yonder 'bout thirty feet from the shack," Hobson motioned as the two men entered the yard. "Nooley were a real big man an' I couldn't drag him far."

"Show me exactly where you buried him."

"Over thar where you see them stones piled up. Put him away with his boots on. Felt real bad 'bout that. No man wants to die with his boots on."

"I'm real sorry about Nooley, Lester. You been together long?"

"Nope, he was the last one Seth hired, 'bout two year ago. Didn't know nothin' 'bout sheep herdin' so Seth put him with me to learn him the ropes."

Morgan was in a quandary. He needed to fill Hobson in on why he came to talk and get some answers to questions that might be helpful in solving the ram mystery. On the other hand the man had just buried his partner. Morgan decided to get on with it.

"Lester, Seth is dealing with a real big problem. Over the last two years, he's been losing rams at a pretty good rate."

"What you mean losin' rams? How you gonna lose rams? You sayin' they runned off, or they got stole?"

"That's what we need to find out. If we don't get to the bottom of this, Seth will be out of business in a couple of years. He won't have the number of sheep needed to make a profit if he doesn't get enough replacement lambs."

"Yeah. Gotta have a bunch a rams to keep them ewes happy, or that'll be a bad thing."

"A real bad thing, Lester."

"Well, I sure don't know what to say. We take our turns lookin' after the rams, but I ain't never seen none disappear. Could be when the Judas goat leads 'em to new grass or to frolic with the ewes that some would stray off, but that ain't likely with the dogs holdin' all of 'em close an' tight."

"How about the times the crews rotate? How long are the rams unattended?"

"Depends on whar the new team's comin' from. Could be a day—could be two. We count on the dogs to do the lookin' after 'til we show up."

"Thanks, Lester, you've been a big help. I'll head back to the house tomorrow and let Seth know what happened out here—that Nooley's dead. I'll try to get some help for you as quick as I can. Since you had this trouble with someone stalking around, I may pull a man off another team to come out."

"Ain't nothin' you needs to do. I'll be okay. I reckon I'd just as soon be alone."

"With this trouble, I think it's best for you to have some backup. I'll get one of the fellows working closest to the house to come out. Could be here day after tomorrow."

"Well, you be the boss. Just make sure you don't send that Injun out. I ain't workin' with that Injun."

"What's the problem between you and Swift Eagle? You were about to go at it during Sunday's meeting."

"That goes way back. Doesn't care to talk on it. Just keep him away from me."

"All right, Lester, that's a promise. Now I'd best get on the trail. I'll spend the night in the empty crew shack the next fold over and leave early in the morning from there. I'll be getting someone out here."

"Don't waste yer time goin' to number fourteen. Water's gone bad at fourteen. Number seventeen'll do you lots better."

"Thanks for the advice. But I'll likely make a quick stop by fourteen to see if I can find out what's wrong with the well."

Finding Nooley had been killed put a big kink in Morgan's plan for his three days on the range; but the death had to be reported and help found for Lester. Lester's reaction to Morgan's observation about Swift Eagle made Morgan more than a little curious about the bad blood between the two. He hoped Swift Eagle would be more willing to talk about whatever had happened.

Morgan also gave serious thought to Lester's report that the water had gone bad at fold fourteen. Seth must not have known of that turn of events or he would have mentioned it. Could the situation of the missing rams be escalating to someone poisoning the wells? Was the person responsible for trying to put Ruddell out of business getting impatient with the pace he'd set? Was he becoming more aggressive?

It was a two-hour ride at a leisurely trot from Lester's fold to number fourteen and another two hours from fourteen to seventeen, where Morgan would spend the night. His trail-weary backside was telling him to go no farther than fourteen. He had enough good water in his canteen to last and his gelding was finding water in the streams along the way. Fourteen had been vacant long enough for new grass to be there for the horse.

Within a mile of reaching his first destination, Morgan noticed buzzards circling over the south side of the fold's fence. He headed in that direction before moving toward the crew shack. Nearing a stand of cottonwoods, he saw a band of four coyotes digging in the ground. He pulled his Winchester from its scabbard and fired two quick shots to scatter the coyotes, then moved into the trees. Sticking out from a mound of earth, he saw a boot gnawed through by the coyotes, a bloody foot inside.

Morgan quickly moved to the mound and scooped away the loose dirt with his hands, uncovering the body of a large man. With some effort he was able to pull the man from the shallow hole. Underneath the body was a hat. Printed in ink on the sweatband was a name: Nooley.

Morgan's mind raced with confusion and anger. Hobson had lied through his teeth. Nooley didn't die from an intruder's bullet. Hobson was the murderer and faked the grave at his fold. Why would Hobson kill his partner of two years and make up such an elaborate cover story?

Morgan put Nooley back in the hole and hurriedly covered him with a thin layer of dirt. If the coyotes and buzzards got to him, so be it. Nooley couldn't be any deader, and Morgan couldn't waste time. He had to get back to Hobson fast, so he pushed the gelding as hard as he possibly could. When they reached Hobson's shack, the horse was lathered.

Even before entering the shack and finding most of the supplies gone, Morgan knew Hobson was nowhere near. And he had no plan to return.

Chapter Six

Clemet Morgan spent an uncomfortable night in the crew shack Hobson and Nooley had called home for two years. The sheep were restless, which made the dogs restless, somehow sensing there was a problem.

The dogs were especially high strung and confused. Good sheep dogs thrive on attention that comes when they do a good job. When rewarded with words of praise or extra treats, they'll work even harder to please. These dogs had been alone for hours; it could be days before they would know whom they were supposed to please next. The best Morgan could do was tie the dogs within reach of water, and leave a washbasin filled with dry dog food so they wouldn't starve.

His horse seemed recuperated from the hard ride back, so after he was fed a good portion of oats and Morgan was satisfied the gelding was sound, they started trekking toward the ranch house. The morning was crisp and chilly, and Morgan wished the sun would quit playing its stalling game and peek over the top of the mountains sleeping in predawn purple to the east. When his wish was fulfilled, the landscape to the west came alive with hues of red, then orange, and finally brilliant yellow, as the full face of the sun smiled brightly through wisps of soft clouds.

The cadence of the horse's hooves hitting the ground was soothing to Morgan, giving him familiar background noise for thinking. Had it been only eleven days since he had pulled into Red Mountain, tired and dirty from being hounded by the Bartonville posse? It seemed longer. He had met some good folks and had come across at least one questionable person. However, the good far outnumbered the bad. Morgan was starting to feel comfortable with where he was and what he was doing to help Ruddell and Millie. Comfortable but not yet at home. Maybe Lorna Porter could take him to that level.

It was almost noon when fold number one came into view. Morgan was heading there for two reasons. It was closest to the ranch house, so when he sent one of the men from that fold to tend Hobson's and Dooley's flock, the man left alone would be close in. Also, the men at number one were Harry Samuels and Swift Eagle, both of whom Morgan felt he could trust.

Both Harry and Swift Eagle had met Morgan, nonetheless he tied the white flag to his rifle, waving it above his head as he rode toward the holding pen. Samuels saw the signal and galloped out.

"I swear, Clemet," Samuels said with a grin, "sure didn't take long to git hired on. Now you be runnin' the whole shebang. Swift Eagle told me 'bout the Sunday meetin'. Said Seth looked real crippled up. Seems like you come along just in time to lend a hand."

"Maybe! There's a whole lot of work to do and lots happening; some not good. Let's find Swift Eagle. I need to talk with you both."

Seeing Swift Eagle's large frame along the fence line, Morgan again waved the white flag to get Swift Eagle's attention. Within minutes, the three were sitting in the crew shack.

"Wish I knew where to start," Morgan confessed.

"Old Navajos say start journey with first step and other foot will follow," Swift Eagle offered with a smile.

With that encouragement, Morgan walked them through the events of the past week, leading up to yesterday, one step at a time. The only part he left out was Ruddell's letter asking him to come to Red Mountain.

"Now, here's some real bad news. No need to beat around the bush. Jed Nooley's dead. From what I've seen, it looks like Lester Hobson's the killer."

The two men sat in stunned silence looking, first at the floor, then at each other, waiting for someone to speak.

"No. I not believe," Swift Eagle finally uttered in a soft voice.

"But, it's true. I saw his body, and I saw a hat with his name in it. It was Nooley all right."

"I believe Nooley dead. I not believe Hobson be killer."

"No one else could've done it, Swift Eagle. Hobson lied about when and where Nooley was killed. He told me someone in the night shot Nooley at their fold and that he buried Nooley the next morning. He even faked up a grave. Then he tried to throw me off the track to keep me from going to where Nooley was really killed. After that, Hobson cleaned out the crew shack and vamoosed. If he's not the killer, he's going to a lot of trouble making people think he is."

"I not believe Hobson be killer," Swift Eagle said firmly. "Hobson not always good. But he not killer."

"Well, try telling that to Jed Nooley," Morgan responded, ending the topic of Nooley's murder, at least for that conversation.

"I need one of you to go out to number sixteen and tend the flock that Hobson left stranded," Morgan said, trying to sound like a ramrod. "Don't matter to me who, but one of you needs to get out there pronto."

"I go," Swift Eagle said immediately. "I go now. I be there before sun go to bed."

"Thank you for that, Swift Eagle," Morgan said sincerely. "You'll need to take some grub. Hobson carried off almost everything. I don't know from where, but I'll try to hire some help real quick so you won't be out there alone."

Riding on toward the ranch house, Morgan tried to frame the conversation he would have with Seth Ruddell. Hobson had been with Seth for ten years. It was apparent, even when they had their Sunday disagreement, they had respect for each other. Telling Ruddell that Hobson killed Nooley, then lied about it and ran away, would be hard for Morgan.

Arriving before supper, Morgan found Ruddell sitting in a chair on the front porch, smoking a pipe. His bad leg was stretched out in front of him to keep it from bending. He was surprised to see Morgan ride in and tie his horse to the hitching post.

"Seeing you back so soon after you left don't seem like a good thing," Ruddell said slowly. "What's the problem, son?"

Morgan slumped into a chair next to Ruddell, sighing deeply.

"There's been a killing, Seth. Jed Nooley's dead."

"Nooley? How did it happen? Where? Why? Do you know?"

"I can give you the 'how' and the 'where' but I sure don't know the 'why.' "

Morgan briefed Ruddell, ending with his conclusion that Hobson was the killer.

"Just can't imagine Lester killing anyone, let alone his partner. They seemed to get on pretty good. Sure, Lester can be ornery as all get out, but Nooley'd learned to look past that."

"Tell me about Nooley."

"Not much to tell. He came riding in one rainy day a couple of years ago, looking for work. Lester's old partner had just quit to head for Arizona, so I put Nooley with Lester and they've been together since."

"The two never had any trouble getting along?"

"Not that I know of. Hard to tell what goes on out there in the folds, though. About the only time I see everyone together is at shearing time. Then we're all so busy from dawn to dark there's no time for arguing."

"Anyone else Lester hung out with?"

"In all the years I've known the man, I can't recall he ever had a real friend; or a real enemy for that matter. That's what makes it so hard to believe that he'd kill Nooley and run off."

"Sorry, Seth, but I have to work with what I know. And there are two things I know right now: Nooley's dead, and Lester's on the run."

"Yeah, that does look bad for Lester. Do you have some ideas about what we do next?"

"I need to get into Red Mountain and report this to the sheriff. I know he can't do much, but he's the law in these parts and it's best to go by the book. And we've got to find a way to let everyone know to be on the lookout for Lester.

"I think this killing makes it so we best come right out with the whole story of what's been happening to you. Not only about the rams, but the craziness that went on the other night. If there's a lunatic running around, we owe it to people to let them know."

"That makes a heap of sense to me, Clemet."

During his ride into Red Mountain the following morning, Morgan tried to piece together anything that might give him a handle on what was going on. No two things seemed to relate. It was difficult enough to look for answers as to what might be happening with the rams—but that part was beginning to look the easiest. This case was shaping up to be the most difficult Morgan had ever tackled.

Reaching Red Mountain, Morgan went directly to the general store rather than Sheriff Gainer's office.

When he walked inside, Amos Porter—who was also looking for the sheriff—greeted him.

"Hey, Clemet! Don't know what brings you to town, but I'm glad you're here. Millie got another real bad scare yesterday. I'm hoping the sheriff will give that Tommy Hunt a good talking to."

"What happened?" Morgan asked quickly, feeling his anger rise. "Is Millie okay?"

"She seems to be fine now, but yesterday when she and Lorna got home from Al's place she was all shook up. When Millie went to milk the cow, that Hunt kid trapped her between him and a stall and got rough with her. Lorna was in the yard with Al's kids and heard Millie screaming. Lorna ran to the barn, grabbed a pitchfork, and backed Tommy down. When Lorna and Millie were running toward the house, Al came riding in and Tommy took off like a shot."

"That poor girl. What else is going to happen to her? Did Millie go back out there today?"

"No. And neither did Lorna. She told Al she wouldn't be back so long as Tommy's around. I thought if the sheriff took a ride out there to talk with Al and Tommy together, the boy might see what he did was something really bad."

Before Morgan could explain his reasons for being in town the sheriff walked in. Morgan listened as Porter retold the story.

"Guess I better go and put a little scare of the law into that lad," Gainer said. "He always struck me as being younger than his years; but I never thought he'd get this carried away."

Morgan started to tell the sheriff that he'd be happy to go talk with Tommy but thought better of it. As angry as Morgan was about Millie being hassled, he had his own problem to report. Ruddell's situation and events of yesterday with Nooley and Hobson needed to be discussed. Morgan suggested he, Porter, and Gainer go to the sheriff's office to talk in private.

Once there, Morgan laid it all out: who he was, why he was there, Ruddell's missing rams, the frightening episode at the ranch house, the murder of Nooley, and Morgan's reasons for thinking the killer had to be Hobson. He saw no need to mention the killing in Bartonville. This was a separate situation requiring another talk.

After listening to Morgan's news, Potter and Gainer

looked at each other, then into space, and finally at Morgan. They were both trying to absorb what they were hearing but struggling with it. Morgan could feel the atmosphere in the small office getting heavy.

"What's happening to our little community?" Mayor Porter wanted to know. "Folks move here because they want to get away from the problems of Santa Fe or Albuquerque. And then this! What's happening isn't good."

"Well Clemet, where do we go from here?" Sheriff Gainer wanted to know. "How do we handle all this?"

"We need to get everything out in the open. Call a meeting of all the folks from miles around. The three of us can share what we know and try to explain what we see happening. Almost nobody knows me, but you two are pillars of the community. Folks respect you. Maybe we should ask the preacher if we could hold a meeting at the church after Sunday's sermon. We could reach some people that way."

"I have a better idea," Porter offered. "Not everyone goes to church. But no one ever misses the annual Harvest Festival that's coming up a week from Saturday. Me and the sheriff can let people know—and I'll get the town council to spread the word—that there'll be a meeting at the end of the fun and games."

"Sounds good to me," Morgan said. "What do you think, Sheriff?"

"That just might work. It's worth a try. One thing we don't want to let happen though. People around here aren't used to these kinds of problems. Let's make sure they don't think you brought them when you came to town."

Chapter Seven

As soon as Sheriff Gainer rode off to give Tommy Hunt some lessons in manners, Clemet Morgan and Amos Porter headed for the Porters' house to check on Millie and, if Morgan's luck held, see Lorna. In all that had transpired the past few days, Morgan's mind still found time for Lorna.

Nearing the house, the two men saw Lorna and Millie sitting in the porch swing, talking intently. As the men got close, Millie ran quickly to Morgan and rushed into his arms, sobbing. This man who had been her rescuer in Bartonville, now holding her shaking body, needed to assure Millie that everything would be all right; that this trouble would end quickly; that one day this would be past and forgotten. However, all he could say was, "I'm sorry" over and again until she took a deep breath and stepped back.

"It's been a nightmare for her," Lorna said. "She didn't sleep a wink last night and hasn't eaten a bite all day. That little snake Tommy Hunt needs to be horsewhipped."

"Sheriff Gainer's on his way to the Alawanda right now to have a sit-down with Al and the boy," Porter said. "Hopefully that'll bring an end to it."

"Al had better believe I'm not going near his place so long as Tommy's there," Lorna said emphatically. "He can bring the children into town for me to look after, but I don't fancy being within twenty miles of that crazy boy."

Lorna took Millie inside to see if Millie could relax enough to sleep. Having seen Morgan, she seemed much calmer and almost eager to find a bed. Porter excused himself to go back to the livery, with a promise that he and the sheriff would get their heads together on a plan for the community meeting. In a few minutes, Lorna came back to the porch.

"I'm sure glad you came when you did. Millie needs to know she's not alone in this thing."

"Seems to me you did a good job of taking care of her. Remind me to never tangle with you, especially when you've got a pitchfork in your hands." Morgan chuckled.

"It's not the same. Women like to know there's a man close by—one who'll be there when he's needed. Other than Seth, I don't think Millie's ever had that. I could be wrong, though, because when I ran into the barn, she was screaming at Tommy to stop pawing her, and yelled something about 'the last man who did that is dead.'

"After Tommy left I asked her what she meant. She

said she was only trying to scare Tommy into stopping. I'm not sure I buy that explanation."

"I'd best be heading back to the Rocking Ewe," Morgan said quickly. "Tell Millie to stay here for a few days longer. I'll bring more of her things when I come on Saturday."

"Don't bother bringing clothes. I've more than enough for both of us, and we're about the same size."

Walking back to the general store to get his horse, Morgan was amused with the realization that size and shape are two different things.

Problems aside, there was a ranch that needed running, and it was Morgan's job to run it. This was not something he'd bargained for when he set out for Red Mountain three weeks before. The job was cut and dried then, dealing only with finding some missing rams. Maybe the thing Morgan should have done following the incident with Chad Barton was head back to Pueblo. Now he was in too far to pull out. He liked most of the people he had met and admired their determination to make something good happen in this vast deserted corner of the world. But at what price? Everyone was working hard to make a go of it. Farmers scratch the arid earth to grow crops; miners dig and blast mountainsides searching for coal or copper; and true-grit ranchers like Seth Ruddell fight cold winters and hot summers for their livestock to make ends meet. Whatever Morgan needed to do to help, he would do.

A mile before getting to the fork in the road, with one

branch heading south to the Alawanda, Morgan dismounted to let his horse drink from a stream that babbled down from the hills through a stand of mesquite. Then the quiet of a tranquil autumn afternoon was shattered by the crack of distant rifle fire. One shot, one dead deer, Morgan figured.

After letting the gelding drink his fill, Morgan mounted and cantered down the road, hoping to reach the Rocking Ewe in time for supper. With all that was going on he hadn't taken time to eat. He made a mental note to always carry some food in his saddlebag, especially if he was to spend much time on the road.

Up ahead in the distance, Morgan saw what appeared to be a horse without a rider, walking toward him. He slowed the gelding so as not to spook the other horse. When they were fifty yards apart, Morgan realized the horse did have a rider, slumped in the saddle. As they came alongside, Morgan grabbed the reins of the horse and pulled it to a stop. It was only then Morgan recognized the rider. It was the listless body of Sheriff Gainer. He had been shot in the back.

Morgan quickly dismounted and pulled the sheriff gently to the ground, laying him in a patch of grass. Gainer's eyelids fluttered briefly, then opened. He seemed to recognize Morgan before closing his eyes for the last time and whispering, "Tell Nellie I love her."

Then he was gone. This gentle store clerk, this reluctant lawman, this loving husband and pillar of the community was dead—shot in the back by a craven assassin. The tin star he wore out of a sense of responsibility and service to the community was still in place on his shirt. In his haste to do his duty, he had pinned it on upside down.

Clemet Morgan's sorrow soon turned to rage. As he wrapped the sheriff in his bedroll and hoisted the limp body across Gainer's saddle, Morgan was so angry his mind refused him space to think. During his entire time in Red Mountain, Morgan had been confronted with questions. Where are Ruddell's rams? What crazy person was roaming around scaring people? Why would Hobson kill his partner and run away? Now, most perplexing of all: Who murdered Harold Gainer? He needed a plan to find the answers.

Morgan knew he shouldn't ride directly into town leading a horse with a body over the saddle. A mile from Red Mountain he removed the sheriff, laid him in a grove of cottonwoods, and tied his horse securely to a tree. After taking care that Gainer was well hidden, he rode hard to the outskirts of town then slowed to a walk until reaching the livery stable.

Amos Porter was visibly shaken and overcome with grief by the news of his friend's death, but realizing they had a job to do, quickly composed himself. He and Morgan hitched two draft horses to the hay wagon and returned to the cottonwood grove to retrieve the sheriff's body and his horse.

Returning to Red Mountain, they decided the best action was to take Gainer's body to Porter's house. They would ask Lorna and her mother to carry the sad news to

Nell Gainer. At the house they pulled the wagon around back and went inside. Porter sent his two boys to close up the livery then explained to the women what had happened.

Millie took it the hardest. She blamed herself for Gainer's death because he was on the road to talk with Hunt when he was killed. Morgan tried to comfort her. He told her the sheriff was doing his sworn duty and he knew the dangers that came with the job. By the time the men brought the body into the house and placed it on the kitchen floor, Millie was calmer.

Elsie Porter didn't want Nell Gainer to see her husband lying on the floor in a blood-soaked shirt. She and Lorna removed his shirt, washed away the blood, and dressed him in one of Porter's bright calicos. The men moved Harold's body to a bed.

Elsie Porter asked everyone to kneel at the sides of the bed and pray before she and Lorna set out on their sad mission. They drove the wagon so they could bring Nell back to the house.

After what seemed an eternity, the women returned. Elsie Porter held onto Nell Gainer tightly as she led the sheriff's widow into the bedroom. Those in the parlor heard Nell moan softly and say, "I love you. How I love you, you old coot." Then Elsie left the bedroom and quietly closed the door, leaving Nell alone to say good-bye to her husband of forty-two years.

The nearest undertaker was in Bartonville. When

someone died in or near Red Mountain, the families of the deceased were expected to do the burying. It would be no different for Harold Gainer. Morgan and the Porter boys drove the wagon to the general store, selected the best pine boards in the store's lumberyard, and quickly, but carefully, built a sturdy coffin.

Back at the house, the sheriff was wrapped in a large cotton blanket and placed in the pine box. Nell Gainer touched Harold's face one final time before Morgan nailed on the lid. Then began the slow, somber journey of a widow and close friends riding in a wagon, carrying the body of a good man to his final resting place.

Harold had told Nell many times that when he died he wanted to be buried in their backyard, underneath the branches of a large oak tree they planted as a seedling. Although he attended church with Nell regularly, he didn't consider himself religious and made it clear he didn't want any service held on his behalf.

Two men and two boys shared the job of digging a grave. Then, by lamplight, the sheriff was lowered into the hole, his badge placed on top of the coffin. Nell threw in a handful of dirt and the others followed her lead. Then the men and boys closed the grave.

Although the hour was late, no one expected to get any sleep. The Porter boys were sent home with an admonition from their father to say nothing to anyone about Gainer's death. They needed a plan before daybreak for letting customers of the general store know why the business was closed. Morgan suggested hanging a sign on the door simply saying "closed until further notice." Lorna argued a message like that would raise too many questions. As the heartbeat of the community, people counted on the general store being open during its posted hours.

"Let's just say what happened," Lorna said. "The store is closed due to the untimely death of Harold Gainer. We will reopen as soon as possible."

"I like that," Nell said. "That's what Harold would want. I just need a day or so to get my wits about me and I'll be fine. I need to keep busy."

"Count on me to come every day and help out," Elsie offered. "I don't know much about clerking, but I can learn fast. And the boys can pitch in too."

"That'll work," Morgan said, responding to Lorna's idea. "If people start asking for more details, let's say Harold was out for a ride and died suddenly. Folks will want to know how he died, but they can be told that at the community meeting we'll be having in a few days."

"My word," Porter sighed, shaking his head. "Things are getting stranger by the hour. Who knows what'll come along next?"

Chapter Eight

It didn't take long for Amos Porter's question to be answered. Shortly after the discussion ended, Clemet Morgan left the Gainer house, concerned about being away from the Rocking Ewe for almost two days. The gelding was tied to the wagon out back, and Lorna walked with Morgan to get him. Neither of them spoke. Just before mounting, Morgan took Lorna's hand and gently kissed it.

As he rode toward the Rocking Ewe the moon was full, giving enough light for Morgan to see the road thirty yards ahead. The sun would be coming over the mountaintops soon, and this terrible night would finally be over. Morgan was mentally and physically fatigued but knew he couldn't sleep until this new day ended. Things were a real mess and it seemed Lester Hobson was to blame for most of it. If

Morgan was right, when Hobson ran after killing his partner, he saw the sheriff on the road and mistakenly thought Harold Gainer was looking for him. Hobson killed the sheriff and headed for Mexico, running away from two murders.

Morgan needed coffee, and lots of it. If Seth Ruddell was true to schedule, Morgan would find a pot steaming on the stove. He urged his horse to go faster but soon realized the poor beast must be as tired as Morgan, so he slowed down. Smoke swirling from the ranch house chimney was a welcome sight.

Knowing Ruddell was probably still jumpy from the scare he and Millie had two nights before, Morgan approached the house with caution. When he felt he was within earshot, he shouted as loudly as he could to identify himself. After the third try, the front door opened and Ruddell hobbled onto the porch, holding his rifle at the ready. When Morgan was close enough to be recognized, Ruddell lowered his weapon and let out a sigh of relief.

"Oh, lordy, Clemet, I'm glad you're back. Did you talk to the sheriff? Will he be able to help us?"

"Let's have a cup of coffee, Seth. I've got a lot to tell you."

Morgan scarcely knew where to begin, so he started with the worst part.

"Sheriff Gainer's dead. He was shot in the back yesterday returning from a visit to the Alawanda. We buried him last night."

Before he was finished with the details as to why

Gainer had gone to see Al Robertson, a rider sped into the yard, dismounted, and ran to the ranch house door. It was Ben Clark, one of the herders.

"Seth! We got some real big trouble out there," Clark said excitedly. "All the rams are gone from number eleven—every last one of 'em. Timbo an' me was goin' there on the rotation an' we could see even before we got close that the fold was empty. A big section a' the pen got pulled down, an' the gate through the barbed wire was tied open. Them rams musta been stampeded through the gate an' are prob'ly scattered all over tarnation by now. The dogs are gone too."

"So it's finally come to this, has it?" Ruddell's eyes burned with anger.

"What're we gonna do?" Clark asked. "Timbo's really spooked an' talkin' 'bout quittin' an' I gotta say that's on some other minds too. Most a' the boys been told that Jed Nooley was gunned down. Now with this happenin' . . ."

"Who knows about the ram stampede?" Morgan asked.

"Just me an' Timbo an' Harry Samuels. We bunked with Harry last night. Timbo stayed out there this mornin'. Harry don't know what's goin' on neither, but he ain't gonna run. He made that real clear."

"I pray to heaven no one runs," Ruddell said. "We're going to need every last soul, and then some, to get through this. We'll go ahead with tomorrow's meeting, but keep the stampede under your hat if you see any of the other men. Tell Timbo to stay with Harry and you go on out to number sixteen and partner with Swift Eagle. I don't want anyone to be by himself."

"You got it, boss," Clark responded, downing the last of his coffee and heading for the door. "An' I don't know what the others might decide; but I'm stayin on."

"Thanks, Ben. That means a lot."

Back in Red Mountain, Mayor Amos Porter decided he needed to call an emergency meeting of the town council right away. With Harold Gainer dead, no one was in charge of keeping the law; and from all that was going on, someone needed to be. Porter sent his two boys riding out to the farms of three council members and he got in touch with the fourth, Reverend Grassley, pastor of the community church. The meeting was set for one o'clock in the sheriff's office.

Having gone to the general store to buy groceries earlier in the morning, the pastor had seen the notice of Gainer's death and he and his wife visited with Nell to give her comfort and support. This freed time for Elsie Porter to go home for a while to freshen up and change clothes. She returned to Nell's house just as the Grassleys were leaving.

"Really, Elsie, you don't have to be here with me," Nell said. "I know you have things to do at home."

"Nothing that can't wait," Elsie replied. "If you need to talk, I'm a good listener. Sometimes talking is a good thing."

Being encouraged to talk was what Nell needed. Over the next two hours she recounted much of her life with Harold Gainer: happy times and sad. But mostly happy. They met in Omaha when they were in their early twenties and married soon after. Harold worked in his father's mercantile alongside his older brother until their widowed father died. The brother sold his share of the store to Harold and moved to Kansas.

Nell helped manage the store until her difficult pregnancy kept her bedridden for much of the time. When she finally delivered, one of their twin girls was stillborn, and the other lived less than a week. To cope with the tragedy and retain their sanity, they agreed they needed to move to a new place.

After selling the mercantile for a good price they set out for Phoenix, with a layover in Durango. It was there fate intervened. As Harold was nosing around Durango, asking merchants questions about the mercantile trade in that part of the country, he was overheard by a ruddy-faced farmer who introduced himself as being from a small New Mexico town called Red Mountain. The only thing Red Mountain needed to make it the perfect place to live, the farmer said, was a general store.

Harold and Nell had dinner with the man, a large Norwegian named Sven Olson, and by the end of the meal they decided to head for Red Mountain, with Olson leading the way. They bought a wagon and two draft horses, filled the wagon with enough supplies to get their business started, and arrived in Red Mountain a week later.

Nell was smiling through a stream of tears as she shared her story. At its end, Elsie gave Nell a warm hug and went into the kitchen to make tea, thinking all the while that once again she was reminded it's not buildings or businesses that make a community. It's the people.

Promptly at one o'clock Mayor Porter called to order the emergency meeting of the Red Mountain town council. As always, Reverend Grassley opened with a prayer for guidance and wisdom. For this meeting they would need a good helping of both.

Porter was determined to lay it all out, starting with the murder of the sheriff. Looks of disbelief and consternation were on each face as he explained the reason Gainer was out on the road, wearing his badge. Next he told about the killing of Jed Nooley and the suspicion that Lester Hobson was responsible. Gainer's death could have been caused by either Hobson or Tommy Hunt. Hunt was probably the last person the sheriff confronted. By the time he shared the story of the harassment of Seth Ruddell and Millie at the Rocking Ewe every head was shaking in disbelief.

"What in the loving world is going on?" asked John Bundy, who came down from repairing his barn roof to attend the meeting. "We've never had even one killing around here. Now we've got two."

"And this thing that went on out at Seth's place is just plain spooky," said Jim Leklem, a local pig farmer.

"There's more to tell," Porter continued. "The problem

Seth's having started more than two years ago when he found a lot of rams missing from his herd. He tried to figure out what was going on, but when more went missing this summer he knew he needed help. He sent for a private detective out of Pueblo, and that man got here a couple weeks ago. His name's Clemet Morgan and he's being introduced around as Seth's new foreman. Let's keep it that way for now."

"Seems to me this whole mess has to do with Ruddell," Leklem argued. "Why ain't he here to give us some answers?"

"Seth had a bad accident and he's laid up. Anyway, he doesn't have any answers. That's why he sent for Morgan."

"And what's this Morgan feller doin' about it?" Leklem was becoming agitated. "Ruddell must be payin' him a good chunk of money, havin' him come down from Pueblo."

"He's doing all he can with what he has to go on. He's a good man. I've spent a bit of time with him and I'm sure he'll get it sorted out. But that aside, we need a new sheriff. Any volunteers?"

Clemet Morgan and Seth Ruddell spent the morning discussing the pros and cons of a scheme to deal with the escalating situation. The most important part of the equation was making certain the rams remaining in the other fold didn't get stampeded. With everything happening so quickly, they weren't even sure anyone was watching those rams. Morgan knew he had to go check.

The second part in creating a stopgap—especially if some of the men would be quitting—was to consolidate all the sheep into one central location.

This would make feeding difficult, Morgan agreed, but having all the men in the same area would display a show of force, giving the troublemakers second thoughts about pulling any more shenanigans.

In case Morgan didn't make it back in time for the crew meeting, Ruddell said he could handle the difficult discussion that was sure to ensue.

Morgan saddled the gelding and was heading out, but stopped when he saw a wagon coming down the road. As the wagon got closer he could see Lorna Porter holding the reins. Millie sat alongside Lorna. Two horses, saddled and on lead ropes, followed. Both women wore leather pants and jackets. Lorna had a gun belt and holster with a Colt revolver strapped around her waist.

"Well, this is a surprise," Morgan said. "A pleasant one, but still a surprise."

"We knew you wouldn't be able to get to town for the supplies we'll need tomorrow," Millie explained, "so we loaded up and came on out. I was worried about Grandpa being here in the house alone. There was nothing keeping me in town."

"That explains Millie's reason," Morgan said to Lorna. "What's yours?"

"I thought this place needed all the help it can get. I don't know what's going on any more than you do—probably a lot less. I'm here to do whatever I can."

"That's great. I'm sure Millie can use a hand getting ready for tomorrow. Nice seeing you, but I need to get out to the herd."

"By yourself?"

"Well, in looking around, I don't see another man here, except Seth, and he can't ride. So, yep, by myself."

"You don't see another man, for sure. But you're looking right at me. I'll be riding with you."

"The devil you will!"

"The devil I won't!" Lorna replied, imitating Morgan's tone of voice.

"I can't let you do it, Lorna. There's a back-shooter out there somewhere and I won't be able to look after you if there's trouble."

"Back-shooters are cowards," Lorna replied in a matter-of-fact statement. "They'll gun a man if he's by himself but they're chicken to go after two. So, I'll be the one making things safe for you. From a distance we'll look like two men."

Morgan wanted to continue the argument but stopped when Lorna held up her hand, palm forward. "This is the way it is, my friend. We can either ride together—or you can be twenty yards ahead of me—but I'm going."

"Give it up, Clemet," Ruddell chuckled. "Looks to me like you'll be in good hands."

Leaving the yard with Lorna in the lead, Morgan's

mind was telling him that Lorna Porter, at any distance, could never be mistaken for a man.

The two horses ran stride for stride in the easy gait their riders had set. Both were strong mounts and had to be kept under tight reins to keep from running full gallop. If circumstances were different, the day would have been perfect for a couple to be out riding together, but that was not the case. Clemet Morgan was becoming more perturbed by the day. After receiving Ruddell's letter and weighing all the apparent factors, he'd concluded solving this case would be little more than a paid vacation. His partner had good-naturedly chided Morgan about taking on the easy jobs and leaving all the dirty work for him. Morgan would have some real stories to tell when he got back to Pueblo.

Stopping by a cool stream to give the horses a breather and a long drink, Morgan realized he hadn't kept a promise he'd made to himself just a couple of days before: he'd left the ranch house with no food in his saddlebag.

"Sure hope there's some grub in the crew shack," he mentioned to Lorna. "If not, we may be eating hay. But my stomach's so empty, even hay might taste good."

Lorna smiled, walked to her horse, opened the saddlebag and retrieved a loaf of sourdough bread and a wheel of cheese.

"I don't think we'll go hungry," she said, as she pulled a knife from its sheath and began cutting slices of bread and cheese. "Here's another example of why it's good I came along. If the back-shooter hadn't killed you, starvation would have."

Reaching the ram fold just before dark, Morgan was relieved to see the rams were okay. There were no crew or dogs to be seen; however Ruddell warned him not to be alarmed if that happened. Sometimes crews shifting to the ram folds were delayed for one reason or another. Still, Morgan had hoped to find at least one man on duty.

The crew shack was well stocked with provisions. Morgan built a fire in the cook stove while Lorna put together the makings for a pot of coffee. By lamplight they feasted on a can of peaches, two cans of beans, and bread and cheese. During the meal, they talked about a lot of unimportant things. Neither wanted to discuss the problems at hand so they chatted about who they were, where they had been, and what might be waiting for them in the future.

They were both worn out from all they had dealt with for so many hours. Morgan watched as the beautiful young woman cleared the plates from the table. She appeared very fatigued and when she stumbled and lost her balance Morgan rushed to catch her, holding her by the shoulders. In the fading glow of the lamp, Morgan bent down and placed his warm lips on hers and they lingered for a moment in an embrace.

Lorna pushed him gently away and Morgan said softly, "I think I'd better sleep outside tonight."

"Yes," Lorna agreed, "that would be a very good idea."

Chapter Nine

The Sunday meeting at the ranch house wasn't going well. Seth Ruddell tried to keep the discussion low-key. Learning of Jed Nooley's murder was hard enough for the men to grasp; hearing that Lester Hobson—one of their own—was thought to be the killer, hit as a double blow. Questions were flying around the room like fruit flies swarming an apple core.

"Hold on a second!" Ruddell shouted. "Let's have some order. I've told you all I know about the murder. We don't need to waste time rehashing it. I'm sorry Nooley's dead and just as sorry it looks like Lester was responsible. For all the years I've known Lester, never once did I think he could do something like this."

The talking quieted considerably as Millie entered the room and passed around a second helping of sweet cakes.

With his mouth full, one of the men asked the whereabouts of Clemet Morgan. "Is he still working here, or did he move on?"

"Still here," Ruddell answered. "He's out on the range seeing what he can do about another problem."

"What kind of problem?" the man wanted to know. "And what makes you think Morgan can solve it?"

"I'll answer your second question first. Clemet Morgan isn't a drover like I've been saying. He's a private detective out of Pueblo. I sent for him because I need help with a problem that started two years ago. Maybe you've noticed that something's been happening to our ram count. The numbers should have been increasing, but just the opposite is happening. I didn't know what to make of it then—and I still don't—but it looks like someone wants me to go bust."

"That sure seems like a slow way of goin' 'bout it," offered another man.

"I agree. That's why I thought a professional investigator could figure it out and put an end to the problem before it got out of hand. Now, things *are* out of hand. Early yesterday morning, Ben Clark rode in with news that one of the ram folds had been pulled down and the fence gate wired open. Half my ram stock is off into the mountains. I can't spare any of you to go looking for them so Morgan rode out to check the other fold. If those rams are gone, too, I'm really in for it."

Timbo Ryan said, "I don't scare easy, but I been real jumpy since me an' Ben found them rams gone. Add Jed

Nooley bein' gunned an' it don't seem safe 'round here no more. I'm thinkin' it's time for me to move on."

"Before any of you move out, listen to the idea Morgan cooked up. Then anyone who wants to quit can draw what's coming to him today and be gone.

"Here's what we'll do. First, move all the sheep out of the folds and drive them to the center of the range. Fold number nine is closest to center, so that'll be everybody's target. Once they're together, and in as tight as we can get them, we'll control them on horseback and by using all the dogs. Half of you'll work a day shift; the other half a night shift. This way we'll know what's going on all the time, and we'll have safety in numbers."

"That's all well and good," Ryan said. "But I got me a new wife, and she's complainin' I don't get to see her much as it is. I guess I'd best cash out and find me other work. No hard feelin', Seth. It's been real good workin' for you."

"No hard feelings either way, Timbo. Anyone else need to move on? Make up your mind now, because in the morning everyone still on the payroll will start moving sheep."

Two older men, saying they didn't feel up to spending all those long hours in the saddle, cashed out along with Ryan. Millie added up their earnings and paid them off. Ruddell invited the three to stay for dinner that was about to be served. They declined, eager to head for home.

After dinner and dessert, Ruddell gave final instructions to the men who decided to stay. They were to give a report to their partners of the plan to move the sheep and the reasons for moving, prevail upon those who might want to quit to wait until after they helped with the move, and bring with them all the supplies left in the crew shacks, as well as the blankets and mattresses from the cots. Folds nine, ten and eleven would be used for cooking and sleeping.

Two hours after the men left the meeting, Morgan and Lorna rode in with the good news that the other ram fold was intact and the rotation crew had gotten there midmorning. Morgan asked what they should do with the remaining rams.

"We'll just let them run with the ewes." Ruddell sighed. "It's a little early to breed to get spring lambs, but we don't have a choice. With only half the rams we need, those guys will really earn their keep. Send a couple of men to help with the move and keep your fingers crossed."

Hearing three men had quit concerned Morgan. By his calculation they would need more, rather than fewer, hands. Furthermore, if others chose to ride away after the sheep were herded to the middle of the range, the work force shortage would reach a critical stage. They decided Morgan would go to Red Mountain and look for new hires; Ruddell would pay top dollar.

While Ruddell continued talking to Morgan about the meeting, Millie was in the kitchen with Lorna, boiling water for tea.

"So," Millie asked with an impish grin, "how was your outing?"

"Very businesslike, thank you. We had a job to do, and we did it."

"You were out there a long time. What did you find to talk about?"

"Oh, lots of things. He's had a very interesting life and really enjoys his work. But he's terribly frustrated that he can't get a handle on what's going on around here. He says it's turning into the most difficult case he's ever tackled."

"Well, it's refreshing to hear a man admit he doesn't have all the answers," Millie said as she poured hot water into the teapot. "Maybe there's some hope for the world after all."

"I think there might be, too," Lorna replied with a smile. "If more men were like Clem and your grandpa, I'd be sure of it."

"Oh, so it's 'Clem' now, is it? No more 'Mr. Morgan' or 'Clemet?' In all the days he's been around, you're the only person to call him Clem. Are you sure all you did out there was talk?"

Lorna didn't respond. Millie added one more observation, "Why, Lorna Porter, I do believe you're blushing."

Morgan left early in the morning to oversee the roundup. By the time he reached fold number nine some of the nearby sheep had already arrived and were being bunched together. Morgan sent two men to help guard the rams and to tell that crew to hold off until the next morning before bringing the rams. He wanted to make sure all the ewes were in place and settled before the rams arrived.

The timing of this disruption was unfortunate, but not disastrous. Being only a couple of weeks shy of when the rams would normally mix with the ewes, the spring lambing would be on schedule, assuming everything went smoothly. As nothing was normal about this situation, the unknown events would be handled as they came along.

Swift Eagle, alone at the fold Lester Hobson had deserted, was unaware of what had transpired since volunteering for the job. The days were warm and the nights cold and crisp. The dogs worked hard to keep the ewes separated when they argued over which would get the best grass. For the most part, life was good—until just after dawn two days earlier. Then things changed dramatically. Swift Eagle was roused from his sleep by the sound of stampeding animals. Rushing into the shack yard, clad in his long johns, he was surprised to see a large number of sheep running hard outside the barbed wire fence. A single rider, pushing the sheep toward the mountains then veering off, was spooking them into a frantic state. Swift Eagle quickly checked the fold he was guarding and determined the sheep were not his. They could, however, have been from another Ruddell fold. He thought for a brief moment about riding after the stampeding sheep; but fearing the rider might return to play havoc with his flock, he stayed.

In the distance the rider paused for a few minutes, looked back toward the scattering sheep, and moved on. Later in the morning, Swift Eagle rode out a short way looking for signs that might help identify the person causing the stampede. He found the rider's horse had a rear shoe missing.

By late afternoon, Morgan was satisfied the roundup was going well. Much better than he expected. He talked with each man as they came in with their sheep and dogs, being mostly concerned about who might be thinking of pulling out. By early evening four told him they needed to get back to their families, but two of those said they would stay on for a couple of more days.

Ben Clark reminded Morgan that Swift Eagle needed to know what was happening, so Morgan sent Clark to talk with Swift Eagle and help bring the sheep in from that fold. Clark was the youngest member of the entire crew but one of the hardest workers. Clark could always be counted on.

In the bustle going on around him, Morgan almost forgot he was a private detective, not a ranch manager. He became absorbed in the job at hand: creating crew shifts, developing logistical strategies for feeding both men and sheep, figuring rest and sleeping schedules, deciding where outrider guards should be positioned, and wondering what kind of mayhem would be in store when the rams arrived. He felt he was becoming a bona fide ramrod.

However, he couldn't let himself stay off-track for long. He was, after all, in this part of the country to solve a mystery—one now spiraling almost out of control. He knew there were some good men in this bunch of herdsmen who could run the show; men who had worked with sheep for years and knew the trade. Come morning, he would sit down with Harry Samuels and put him in charge.

By late that night all the flocks had been brought in except Swift Eagle's and the rest of the rams. The men drew straws to see who would be the first to sleep. The shifts would rotate every three hours until morning, then increase to six hours. Morgan would spend the entire night on duty, tending the fires and keeping the coffee hot in the three crew shacks.

Knowing he should be planning the next steps in the investigation, he nonetheless wiled away the night with thoughts of Lorna Porter. His leaving the ranch house that morning without saying good-bye seemed more like running away than just leaving early. He knew she would have insisted on going with him and he wouldn't have been able to argue her out of it. Nevertheless, from time to time during the day he had hopes of seeing her ride up.

When morning finally came, Morgan found Samuels and broached the need for Morgan to return to Ruddell's. Samuels was reluctant to assume the job of range boss, but understood why it was necessary. He was the oldest and most experienced of the crew remaining on board and, in Morgan's opinion, the most levelheaded.

As Morgan shared with Samuels his thoughts on crew rotation and guard positioning, Swift Eagle came riding through the heavy mass of sheep like a fish swimming against a current. Morgan and Samuels were surprised to see him in camp so early, and alone.

When Ben Clark had explained to him all that was happening, Swift Eagle knew he needed to get to Morgan quickly to report he had seen the rams stampeded and he'd gotten a distant look at the man responsible.

"Just one man?" Morgan asked.

"Yes. One man, ride fast. Rams all run to mountains. Then man leave. After man go I look for sign. Horse lost shoe on back foot."

"Good job, Swift Eagle. Do you think any of the rams can be found?"

"If I track, I find. I take two Navajos. Then we all track."

Morgan turned to Samuels. "Well, Harry, it's your call to make."

"It looks like a gamble either way," Samuels replied. "We can run a short crew here an' maybe get a bunch of the rams back, or leave the rams be an' have more men here in case they's trouble. If only one man's causin' all this mischief, slim chance he'll come back an' mix with us. The other side of the coin says, the more rams we got, the better."

With that, Samuels made his first decision as manager. He told Swift Eagle to get some rest, pick his two men, and go find as many rams as they could. Two hours later, three Navajos, each carrying a dog, headed toward the mountains.

Chapter Ten

Clemet Morgan, dead tired on his return trip to ranch headquarters, gave the gelding his head to set the pace. Trying to remember the day of the week and time of day the Harvest Festival was scheduled occupied some of his time. There needed to be a better fix on the agenda for the community meeting. After talking it through with Seth and getting together with Amos Porter in Red Mountain, Morgan hoped they would have a plan in place.

The murder of Harold Gainer needed to top the list of discussion items, together with the announcement of the appointment of a new sheriff. Morgan was thinking how people don't appreciate the importance of law enforcement in a community until they find themselves without it.

Swaying along in the saddle, Morgan dozed off for a time. When he shook his mind out of the trance-like state it was in, he was nearing the ranch house. Seth Ruddell was sitting on the front porch, a blanket wrapped around his shoulders, smoking his pipe. He was in such deep thought he didn't hear Morgan's approach. Millie did, however, and when she called a greeting from the doorway, Ruddell jerked.

"Sorry, Grandpa. I didn't mean to give you a start, but Clemet's back from the range."

"So he is, for a fact," Ruddell replied, waving a greeting to Morgan as he neared the hitching post. "Dish him up some dinner, sweetheart. Looks like he could use a good meal under that belt."

"And a bath," Morgan added. "Feels like I've got half of New Mexico sticking to my skin."

While Morgan ate and the bath water heated, Morgan gave his report. Ruddell seemed pleased with the possibility of recovering some of the stampeded rams.

"If anyone can find them, it'll be those Navajo boys," he said. "They've got eyes like hawks and know how to track better than a duck knows how to swim."

"You looked pretty pensive when I rode up, Seth. Something else going on you'd like to talk about?"

"Nothing new. Al Robertson was here this morning. Rode in just as we were sitting down to breakfast, wanting to talk again about buying me out. Said he'd heard about all the problems we're having and opined this might be a good time for me to sell."

"What did he know? Did he spell it out?"

"Claimed he didn't know any details. Just stories he'd picked up here and there from folks he'd run into."

"Did he say who any of these folks might be?" Morgan felt his investigator juices starting to flow.

"Nope. He just used terms like 'word has it' and 'what I hear is' and such. When I told him there wasn't a chickadee's chance in a tornado that I'd ever sell, he got downright testy. Said I was an unreasonable old gas-passer, and there might not be another offer; or if there was, it wouldn't be as good as the one he just made. He got all red in the face and was about to say more except Lorna settled him down."

"Lorna's still here? Where is she? I'd like to have her take a message back to Amos."

"She cut out when Al left. He was heading for town and she decided to tag along."

"Who's tending his kids while he's out running around?" Morgan asked, his voice filled with agitation.

"They're in Bartonville with their mama's parents. Tommy Hunt drove them up right after the sheriff was killed. Al said he wanted them out of the territory until things cooled down. I can't blame him for that."

"No, and neither can I," Morgan agreed.

Morgan stayed in the wooden bathtub on the screened back porch until the water got cold. Lye soap never felt or smelled so good. When he dressed and returned to the kitchen, Millie was sitting at the table sipping tea.

"Hard day?" she asked.

"Yeah, pretty much, but everything seems better now. Thanks for the tub. After about three days of sleep, I'll be good as new."

"Clemet, could I ask you something? You don't have to answer if you don't want to."

"Sure, Millie, you can ask me anything you want."

"Do you find me attractive? Do you think any man would find me attractive?"

Morgan paused to consider where his response might lead, and then answered.

"Yes, Millie, you're very attractive. I thought so when I first met you in Bartonville, and I think so now. Why do you ask?"

"Just a woman thing, I suppose. I see the way you and Al Robertson look at Lorna, and I wish some man would look at me that way. I mean a real man, one who will love me and look after me, and let me look after him. I'm so disgusted with the Chad Bartons and Tommy Hunts of the world. After what happened the other day with Tommy, I don't want to ever see him again."

"Well, Millie, I know for sure there's a real good man out there just waiting for you to come along. Be patient until he finds you."

Although not having a full night's rest for more than three days and wanting uninterrupted sleep, Morgan hardly made it through the night. When he woke for the last time, he spent the better part of a half-hour staring at the barn loft. His first impulse was to saddle up and head back to the range, but reasoned Harry Samuels had everything under control. Going to Red Mountain and sitting down with Amos Porter to talk about the community meeting was more important.

Morgan found Porter at his shop, repairing a wagon wheel that had lost its metal tread. Even though the morning was cool, the rotund blacksmith was sweating.

"I got lots to tell you, Clemet," Porter said, extending his hand in greeting. "But you go first. What's happening at the ranch?"

Morgan ran through the high points of the past days and ended the review with an observation. "Seth's in a world of hurt—and not just his body. His spirit seems to be in pain as well. He didn't say as much, but when those men who'd worked with him for a long time took a walk, it hit him hard."

"There's no fairness to it. The man has tried all his life to make the best of things and then something like this comes along and drags him down. The same was true for Harold Gainer. Big difference is, Seth's still alive."

"Yes, and I plan to make sure he stays that way."

Porter suggested they sit outside, away from the heat of the forge.

"So what's been happening on this end," Morgan asked.

"Oooo, boy," Porter replied, shaking his head from side to side. "First off, I got the town council together to let them know the real cause of Harold's death. Then I talked about the problem with Seth's rams and Jed Nooley being shot. I told them who you are, why you're in the territory, and that you suspect Lester Hobson of killing both Harold and Nooley. One of the men asked what you planned to do about it."

"We need to keep one thing straight. My job is to find who's playing havoc with Seth. That's it! I work for Seth Ruddell and I take my orders from Seth Ruddell. If my investigation leads me to believe the killing of Harold and Nooley tie into Seth's problem, I'll follow up. Otherwise, it's the job of your new sheriff to start tracking Hobson down."

"Well, sir, that's a problem on its own. As of now, we don't have a sheriff. When Harold served as a member of Red Mountain's first town council, the council decided it needed to give someone the authority to enforce their rules and regulations. The sheriff's job was created and Harold volunteered to take it on. He was the only sheriff this town ever had. At our meeting I asked the council members for a volunteer to stand up and take the oath of office. But we all stayed glued to our chairs, me included."

"This is a heck of a time to be without a lawman. If word gets around, you'll have every bad apple in the territory moving in."

"We talked on that some. The best answer we could come up with was for the town council to be sort of a watchdog group for the area. We'll meet every Saturday until we find a sheriff."

"Let's put this all on the table at the community meeting. Maybe someone will step forward."

"That brings up another wrinkle," Porter added. "One of the council members is Reverend Grassley, the local preacher. I made it real clear that none of us on the council should say anything to anybody. I wanted as many people as possible to find out at the same time what's going on, so I told the men it would be best if it all comes out at the festival meeting.

"I almost fainted and fell back in it Sunday at the church service to hear the good reverend's sermon on the commandment, 'thou shalt not kill.' He used the sermon to spill his guts about almost everything I'd asked him to be quiet about. He told about Harold being killed and prayed for ten minutes asking the Lord to look after Nell. He told about Nooley being murdered and prayed for five minutes that Nooley's soul makes it to heaven. He told about Lester Hobson being the killer and prayed, for who knows how long, that Lester will see the evil of his deeds and find forgiveness in the Lord. Finally, he told us not to worry because there's a man from Pueblo in town named Clemet Morgan, and he'd take care of everything. Then you got prayed over.

"All this would've been fine at another time, except there was only about twenty folks in church, and he'd been told to keep his mouth shut until festival. I asked him afterward why he'd done it. Said he felt it was the Lord's will.

"Just proves my old granddaddy was right when he

told me if you want to get a good gossip fire going, light the first match in a church service."

"Well, it's done," Morgan said with resignation. "Guess we'll have to make the best of it. Let's hope there'll be a good turnout for the festival."

Morgan moved to another subject.

"By the way, Lorna was a great help out at Ruddell's. Know where I can find her? I'd like to thank her again. She left for home before I got back from the range."

"She and Elsie are at the general store giving Nell a hand. I'm sure you'll find her there."

"It was good of Al Robertson to ride in with her."

"I reckon so, but most likely he was headed this way. His horse threw a shoe and he brought her in to have me make a new one. He seemed to be in a big hurry. Kept after me to work faster so he could be on his way."

"Which shoe was missing?"

"Right rear. Why do you ask?"

"Oh, just curious."

Morgan's suspicious, problem-solving mind was running full throttle as he slowly walked the gelding between the livery and the general store. It might have been Al Robertson who released and stampeded the rams. If that's the case, it could also be Robertson was responsible for the disappearance of the other rams over the last two years. No, that didn't jibe. A stampede could have happened anytime before this and would have worked much faster toward putting Ruddell out of business.

What's turned up the heat now? And what, if anything, do the murders of Nooley and Gainer have to do with what's happening? Morgan was so wrapped in thought he almost missed turning on the street to the general store.

When he arrived, Lorna was in front of the building washing the windows.

"I could use a woman like you around my office," Morgan quipped. "Folks complain that when they're inside, they don't know if it's day or night."

"Be glad to teach you how it's done. Grab a rag and have at it."

"Golly, ma'am, I'm much obliged but I got to get on back to the ranch. Just wanted to swing by to see how Nell's doing."

"She's remarkable. She goes to Harold's grave in the mornings, talks to him about the day's schedule, then comes in here and works all day."

Morgan was interested in what Lorna and Robertson had talked about on their ride into town from the Rocking Ewe. There were some things happening that might be helpful to the investigation. Coincidental? Perhaps nothing more.

"Sorry you left before I got back to the house. I didn't want you riding into town by yourself. I was glad to hear Al was visiting Seth and rode in with you."

"I'm sure I would have been just fine. As much as anything, I wanted to ride along with Al to calm him down. He and Seth had a pretty hot discussion."

"So Seth told me. Did Al have more to say about why he was so out of sorts?"

"He had plenty to say. But not much of it made sense. It was more of a diatribe than a discussion. He rambled on about how he'd tried to make it easy on Seth, but his patience was running out. He felt he'd made Seth a fair offer for the Rocking Ewe and couldn't understand why he wouldn't take it. Seth is getting on in years, he said, and may never recover from his accident. Seth should take the offer, then he and Millie could live the good life in Santa Fe or Albuquerque."

"I didn't know Al was wealthy enough to buy Seth out. A spread the size of the Rocking Ewe is worth a pretty penny."

"I think that's another reason Al was so full of vinegar. He claims he has a backer with lots of money who would buy the ranch, combine it with the Alawanda, and lease it back to Al. Problem is, the backer has set a deadline for the deal to happen."

"That must be the reason Al's putting on the pressure. Guess maybe I'll drop by the Alawanda and pay him a visit."

"You can save yourself a trip. He'll be coming to the festival on Saturday. It's probably better if you wait and talk then."

"How can you be sure he'll be there?"

"Oh, he'll be there all right. He told me he'd be bidding on my picnic basket and would go as high as needed to get it. He went so far as to tell me what he wants to eat."

"Guess you need to explain what you mean."

"Of course, you wouldn't know about the festival tradition." Lorna laughed. "One of the main reasons we have the festival is to raise money to help run the school. There's a farmers' market with a lot of donated goods and produce; booths are set up for games of chance; there's a program put on by the students and they pass the hat for contributions.

"But the biggest fund-raiser, by far, is the picnic basket auction. All the women fix picnic lunches for the men to bid on. The winning bidder shares the lunch with the woman who brought it. Husbands aren't allowed to bid on their wives' baskets. It's a lot of fun."

"Sounds like it. Don't be surprised if Al has a bidding war on his hands."

Chapter Eleven

Clemet Morgan was eager to get back on the range. A number of procedures the men were accustomed to had already changed and more needed to be. In the near future there would be no Sunday meetings, an important part of which was distributing supplies for the crew shacks. Now, the supplies would need to be delivered.

As Clem rode in the early morning mist he suddenly had thoughts of Pueblo. One of the last acts Harold Gainer performed before he died was to send a telegraphed message from Morgan to his partner in Pueblo. Morgan alerted Jamison Jakes that he might need help and asked him to be ready to come to Red Mountain on short notice. The fly in the cow pie now was that Harold Gainer was the only telegrapher within fifty miles. Even if Morgan needed his partner's help, he had no way of contacting him or even getting a reply from the message already sent.

Adhering to the order he'd given the men to tie a white cloth to their rifles when nearing the holding compound, Morgan rode into the center of the milling herd with his flag held high. He found Harry Samuels wrapped in a blanket on the floor of crew shack ten and roused him from a deep sleep.

"Sorry, Harry, but I can't stay long. Just came for a quick check. Is Swift Eagle back? Did they find any rams?"

"Brought in thirteen yesterday, all wearin' Seth's paint brand," Samuels replied, rubbing his eyes. "They've gone back to look for others. I told 'em one more day, an' that's it. Otis Marshall took fer home, so we're really in the hurt. Did you find any new hires?"

"No, sorry. The closest I came was Amos Porter's two boys. They all but begged to sign on, but Amos doesn't want them out here in harm's way, and neither do I. How many men are still with us?"

"Twenty-six. I think we can make do with that, but fer how long, I can't tell you."

"Going to have to make do with only twenty-five for a few days. I need one to take the wagon into town for supplies and bring them out here. Who can you spare?"

"Can't spare no one—but I'll give you Ben Clark," Samuels said. "He's young, but he's a scrapper an' really likes workin' fer Seth. Most of all, he can be counted on to come back with the supplies. Some a' the others are so spooked they might turn tail an' run if someone close to 'em sneezes."

"All right, Clark it is," Morgan agreed. "Have him be at the house before dark tomorrow. He can take the wagon on Saturday morning, get the supplies, spend the night at the house, and deliver the goods Sunday."

"Sounds like a plan. I'll see to it that Ben's at the house in time fer supper."

Samuels was true to his word. The next afternoon Ben Clark rode into the yard a few minutes before Millie had the table set. The aroma of smoked ham and hot biscuits filled the air. Clark stood for a moment on the porch, inhaling deeply.

Clark had grown up in Red Mountain until he was eleven. When his father found work in Santa Fe, the family moved. Clark and Millie had attended Red Mountain's three-room school together and many times the Clarks and Ruddells shared a meal, usually on Sunday. After seven years in Santa Fe, Clark came back to Red Mountain. City living was not for him. He rented a room from Maude Lewis, owner of the Good Grub Café, and made due with odd jobs. A year later there was an opening at the Rocking Ewe and Clark eagerly filled it.

Before Clark had a chance to knock on the door, Millie opened it and greeted him.

"I think I remember you," she said blithely. "You used to live around here didn't you? Now rumor has it you work for my grandpa, unless I have you confused with someone else. Is your name Ben something-or-other?"

"Guilty as charged," Clark said, grinning broadly.

"Hurry on in here, boy," Seth Ruddell said in a loud voice, "before all this good food gets too cold to eat."

During supper Morgan tried to keep the conversation light. There would be enough heavy talk at the festival. Morgan did explain, however, in careful detail, what Clark needed to do. Because of the festivities the general store would be closed, but Nell agreed to open long enough for Morgan and Clark to purchase and load the goods needed at the ranch.

Then Morgan made a suggestion. "Ben, why don't you take in part of the festival before you leave town? I hear it's a heap of fun."

"Gosh, thanks Clemet, but I don't cotton much to crowds. I'll just load up an' head on back."

"And do nothing but sit around here and watch me whittle?" Ruddell asked. "You're dumber than a stump, boy. Stay in town and kick up some dust. Besides, Millie needs to ride in the wagon so she can carry her picnic basket. Then she'll need a ride home."

"It's settled then," Morgan announced. "This means I can get in town earlier to meet with Amos and the city council."

As Millie was clearing the supper dishes and Ruddell

shuffled toward the porch to smoke his pipe, Morgan motioned for Clark to follow him to the backyard.

"Ben, I got another favor to ask. Millie's been through a lot of hard times the past few weeks so the festival will give her a chance to take her mind off things. Tomorrow, when the picnic baskets are auctioned off, I'd be much obliged if you'd bid on Millie's. Here are five silver dollars. If you need to spend more, I'll pay you back. If you spend less, keep the difference."

Morgan was up at dawn, and by the time he arrived at the Red Mountain schoolyard, it was already swarming with activity. Some men were putting up concession tables that would soon be loaded with fruits and vegetables, jams and jellies, baked goods, fudge, eggs, handmade arts and crafts, quilts, and potted plants. A number of crates filled with chickens and geese were on the schoolhouse steps. Tied to a tree adjacent to the children's play area, two milk cows were laying in the shade chewing their cuds.

Around the perimeter of the large brown lawn, other men were erecting booths for conducting various games of chance, fortune telling, and weight-guessing. A sweet-looking volunteer, who would be selling her lips, was decorating the kissing booth. A small band, assembled in a grove of trees to practice their tunes, had already attracted an audience.

All this made an impression on Morgan. The event was like an annual family reunion: People greeting one another with handshakes and hugs, backslaps, laughter, and genuine fondness. It brought back nostalgic memories of his Indiana childhood; memories of happy carefree times before getting into the private detective trade in big–city Pueblo.

The sound of Children playing on swings and slides and climbing on monkey bars filled the air. A group of old men commandeered one of the tables and began their cutthroat checkers tournament, the winner to receive a free sample at the kissing booth.

It was hard for Morgan to pull away from soaking in all that was around him, but he knew the mayor and city council would be waiting at the jailhouse. Before he was twenty feet from the building he heard arguing. He quickly opened the door and went inside.

"Here he is now," Mayor Porter announced, with some relief. "Glad you could make it, Clemet."

"Glad to be here. Glad we're getting together to talk about what's going on. We need to agree on an agenda for this afternoon's meeting. We also have to throw some cold water on whatever rumors are milling around." Morgan looked directly at Reverend Grassley.

"That's what we've been discussing," Porter interjected. "We're split on whether to even have a meeting. Seems like most people know something bad is happening, but Leklem, here, and the reverend think enough's been said, and we should let things be. John Bundy and I feel the more that's out in the open, the better. Pete Templer's laid up and won't be coming. So we're split. I don't think any of us will change our minds."

"Well, you're the ones elected to make the decisions," Morgan said with resignation. "Guess I'll never understand politics. Why is it when there's a tie vote, the ones against a plan always get their way? Couldn't the two of you who think it's important to have a meeting go ahead and have it and the other two keep quiet?"

Morgan left the council meeting shaking his head, trying to think of alternate ways the community could be told of the problems without holding a group meeting. As he walked about, a number of citizens introduced themselves, asking if he was the new manager of the Rocking Ewe. Many expressed concern about Ruddell's health and his safety.

It was soon apparent that almost everyone knew the sheriff was dead and that he was killed doing his duty, though there were many versions of what had actually happened. When Nell Gainer showed up, women friends gathered around her to offer condolences.

Nell spotted Morgan and excused herself from the ladies to meet him as he walked toward her.

"Millie and that nice Ben Clark came by earlier. We've filled the order rather than waiting until later. No need for those young people to leave the fun in the middle of the day. The wagon's put away in the shed and the horses are in the corral, so they can hitch up and be on their way whenever they choose."

"That's great, Nell. Millie deserves to have a little fun with someone her own age. Where are they now?"

"We walked over together. Millie had a real nice picnic basket—one of the prettiest I've seen. I hope it does well in the auction."

"I'll be very surprised if it doesn't," Morgan replied with a grin. "Very surprised."

Morgan was looking for two people in particular—Lorna Porter and Al Robertson—hoping he would find them separately, not together. As he stood on the street opposite the jailhouse, the door opened and the mayor and city council members emerged. Leklem and Grassley went quickly into the crowd, their civic duty done for the day. Porter motioned Morgan over. The mayor and John Bundy waited while Morgan hurried to where they were. Then the three went inside.

"We're sorry about the community meeting being scrubbed," Porter said. "But John and me hatched an idea; sort of a compromise." Bundy nodded.

"First off, let me tell you what we talked about after you left. Neither Leklem or the reverend came right out and said it, but the reason they don't want to be a part of any meeting is they're just flat-out scared. Grassley thought he'd done his part, with all the yakking and praying from the pulpit on Sunday. And Leklem came to the meeting with marching orders from his missus to not get involved. She didn't want him to end up like Harold Gainer. Knowing Leklem's wife, he'll do as he's told.

"They both resigned from the council. I made them put it in writing."

"So be it." Morgan sighed. "Another crack in the shell. What's this compromise you've cooked up?"

"It's like this," Porter said. "The event that's the center of attraction at the festival is the picnic basket auction. Everything else stops while that's going on. I'm the auctioneer, so I pretty much control the whole shebang. We're thinking when everybody's there waiting for the first basket to go on the block, as mayor I'll say a few words before the bidding starts."

"That's right," Bundy joined in. "He'll thank everyone for coming to help raise money for the school; you know, pleasantries like that. Then he'll hit them with the bad news about Harold and add enough information to set the story straight, but not so much that they panic."

"One other thing we feel that's important," Porter added, "is for you to be introduced as a professional lawman so you can give your read on what's going on. This'll make people feel more at ease—especially since we don't have a sheriff. How does that sound?"

"I don't have a problem going that direction," Morgan replied. "So long as you make it clear I'm *not* the sheriff and that a new one will be on duty real quick."

"Fair enough," Porter said. "Now let's go have a good time!"

Back on the street, Clemet Morgan was feeling better about the folks in charge of Red Mountain. He understood Grassley and Leklem being hesitant regarding getting involved with the problems the town was facing. Nothing like this had ever come along, this bombshell of murder and robbery. Serenity in a small town is a treasure—a quiet, peaceful heaven on earth—far removed from the crime and grime of larger places. That's why people come here, and stay here. To have that serenity threatened, and possibly destroyed for reasons they don't understand, is a jolt at best.

Morgan was pulled abruptly from his pensive state of melancholy by seeing Lorna, wearing a bright gingham dress and moccasins, engaging in conversation with a group of laughing children. To him she appeared, simultaneously, both out of place and in the exact place she should be.

She seemed out of place because, in the short time Morgan had known her, she had always worn tight-fitting leather or denim pants, long-sleeved shirts, and boots. Very much the lady wrangler. Yet now, with the children, she looked every bit the schoolteacher she hoped to become.

Winding his way through the crowd to say hello, Morgan saw a man approaching Lorna and the children. He realized the man must be Robertson. With a backward wave of his hand, the children ran off to play, leaving him alone with Lorna. Morgan was turning away when she called to him.

"Clemet, hello! Come here. There's someone I want you to meet."

"Oh, hello, Lorna," Morgan answered, feigning surprise.

She waited for Morgan to join them and then made the

introductions. "Clemet Morgan, this is my friend, Al Robertson. Al owns the Alawanda right next to the Rocking Ewe. And, Al, this is—"

"I know who you are," Robertson interrupted. "You're that hombre from Pueblo who's down here to stir up trouble. And from what I hear, you're gittin' the job done!"

"Whoa there, fella. I don't know what you heard, or who you heard it from, but I'm hired to solve problems not create them."

"Oh yeah? Then why'd we git into a whole passel of grief right after you got here? Men gittin' killed and sheep bein' run off never happened 'til now?"

"Interesting you should mention the part about the sheep. I've got a few questions about that situation. Do you have a minute?"

"You can ask all you care to, city slicker, but don't expect answers."

"Stop it, both of you," Lorna said sternly, stepping between the two. "This is meant to be a fun day. Let's keep it civilized."

Morgan grudgingly extended his hand toward Robertson.

"No way," Robertson scoffed. "Not today or any other day."

"Well, I'm not going to let my fun be spoiled by the likes of either of you yahoos," Lorna said, turning her back to both men and heading toward the schoolyard.

Morgan and Robertson glared at each other for a moment. Then Robertson walked away in Lorna's direction.

Morgan stood for a moment, assessing what'd just happened. He concluded he handled the situation poorly. Maybe he was thinking too much about Lorna. The number one rule for conducting an investigation is to never get personally involved in a case. Nonetheless, Morgan was slipping further from that rule every day.

A half-hour before the picnic basket auction, Morgan found a quiet spot to think about what he would say to the crowd after Porter introduced him. Knowing his tendency to give more information than is necessary, he outlined three simple points. First he would thank the mayor for the opportunity to speak. Then he would tell the folks how much he enjoys their community. Finally he would give his "read on things" as Bundy had suggested.

While Morgan was mulling, two men walked close to where he was sitting. They stopped for a minute and stared at Morgan, then walked slowly away. He had noticed these men earlier in the day as they stood on the periphery of the activity. They appeared to be loners. He had dismissed them as drifters stopping to take in the festival. Morgan's eyes followed the two as they moved away from him, staying to the outside of the crowd. He was more than a little curious when Robertson approached the men. Morgan watched as the three engaged in animated conversation. When the talk among the three ended, Robertson moved back into the crowd, now coming together in front of the school for the start of the auction.

Morgan took a position to the right of the schoolhouse steps and stood looking into the faces of the crowd.

Feeling a deep appreciation for this annual tradition, he was reminded how important it was for him to get everything back to normal.

All the baskets were placed on a long row of tables and the women who prepared the lunches stood behind their creations. The bidding started with the basket closest to the auctioneer and everyone moved down a place as each basket sold. Then the winning bidder and the woman owning the basket would find a spot to eat. All the children had lunch pails and could eat whenever they got hungry. It was indeed a splendid occasion. Although the end of the auction signaled the official closing of the festival, people could hang around for as long as they pleased.

A wooden lectern served as the auctioneer's stand, accompanied by a gavel.

When Amos Porter determined the number of people was sufficient to begin the auction, he gaveled the event to order. As quiet rippled through the eager mass of hungry friends and neighbors, Morgan kept his eye on the two strangers who were standing off to the side near the front of the gathering.

Mayor Porter stood silent for a moment, looking out over the crowd, reflecting on years of happiness and toil, of good times and bad, of welcoming new neighbors and saying farewell to old friends.

He took a deep breath and shouted, "Hello, Red Mountain!"

"Hello, Mayor!" the crowd answered.

"Welcome to the twelfth annual Harvest Festival. It

just gets bigger and better every year. On behalf of the school board and city council, I want to thank you for being here to support the efforts of the school and its teachers. Without your generous donations, we wouldn't have a school.

"I know we're all hungry so we'll be getting to the auction real quick. But first I want to say a few words about some things that have been happening in our community lately that are new to all of us. The saddest is the death of our good friend, Harold Gainer. Harold lived here in Red Mountain for more years than most of us. When he and Nell came to Red Mountain there was a lot fewer of us than now. His general store helped many of us decide to settle here. When we got so big we needed a sheriff, it was Harold who stepped up and took the job. He kept the peace by being smart and wise, not by carrying a gun.

"You all know Sheriff Gainer died last week. But you might not know that he died in the line of duty: Shot in the back out on the trail."

Some people in the crowd nodded their awareness. A few stood in shocked disbelief.

The mayor continued. "We don't know for a fact who the killer is, but we've got a pretty good idea. Keep your eyes open for Lester Hobson, who worked out at the Rocking Ewe. There's a number of reasons Hobson's on the hot seat for murder, so be real careful if you see him.

"Here's a man I want you all to meet. His name's Clemet Morgan and he's down here from Pueblo. He was sent for by Seth Ruddell to see if he could help with a problem Seth's been having. Come on up here, Clemet, so the folks can get a gander at you."

As Morgan approached the schoolhouse steps, the two strangers moved further away from the crowd, disappearing into a grove of cottonwoods.

"No need for Morgan to speak," Porter said, sensing the hungry throng was getting restless, "but if you have any information that might be helpful, he's the man to see. Now, let's get on with the auction."

All the women hurriedly took places behind their baskets. Each of the forty-one baskets had a large number attached. The lunches had been available to any men wanting to lift the lids and inspect the contents. Morgan noted that Millie had been assigned number seven and Lorna, thirty-four. Porter wasted no time in getting the bidding going and within a very few minutes Millie's basket was on the block. Each bid started with a minimum of twenty-five cents.

Ben Clark opened the bidding at two dollars, much to the surprise and glee of many onlookers.

"Two-fifty," came a call from the cottonwood grove as one of the strangers stepped into the clearing, lifting his arm to be recognized. Millie looked toward Ben as he shouted, "Three dollars!"

"Three-fifty," answered the stranger. Millie grew pale.

Clark reached into his pocket and pulled out all the coins he'd been given by Morgan.

Holding high his fist full of money, Clark yelled, "Five dollars!"

Porter quickly slammed the gavel and said in a loud voice, "Sold for five dollars!"

"Hey, just a gol'durn minute," the stranger said. "I ain't through biddin' yet."

"Sorry, mister," Porter replied. "The rules say there's a five dollar limit for the first ten baskets, and whoever gets there first, wins the bid." Porter winked at Millie and she smiled as Clark handed the silver dollars to Elsie Porter, who was collecting the money.

"That's a crock!" the man said, returning to the cottonwoods.

The bidding that followed returned to a normal flow. Many of the couples who were already eating had found spots close in the schoolyard, some sitting at the tables, others on blankets in the brown grass. Morgan noticed with some satisfaction that Millie and Clark were strolling toward the general store, probably to hitch up the supply wagon. They would share their picnic out in the countryside on their way back to the ranch.

When basket thirty-four was announced, Bundy quickly opened the bidding at fifty-cents, followed by Morgan with one dollar. Robertson, as expected, came in with two dollars, but was countered by Bundy's two-fifty, then Morgan's three. Robertson glared at his two competitors and bid three-fifty. Bundy bid four, and Morgan, five. By now many of the folks nearby stopped to listen; some moved toward the steps.

When Robertson's bid reached six dollars, Bundy looked at Lorna, slowly shook his head and walked away.

Porter raised his gavel to close the bidding, but Morgan wasn't finished.

"Ten dollars!" he said loudly, glaring back at Robertson, whose anger was apparent.

"Twelve dollars!" Robertson snarled, stepping into Morgan's space. Morgan looked at Lorna, who held up her hands in a stopping gesture, shaking her head, telling him to leave it be. Porter could see the distress on his daughter's face.

"The auctioneer bids thirteen dollars," Porter said quickly. "Going, going, gone! Sold to the auctioneer, for thirteen dollars!"

Lorna carried her basket to the steps, whispered something to her father, kissed him on the cheek and walked in the direction of her house. Morgan thought for a very brief moment about following her to apologize for creating a situation that could have turned ugly.

In his thirty years, Morgan had never had much luck in relationships with women. There hadn't been many, and only one he considered serious. Soon after arriving in Pueblo, he met a woman who came close to being everything Morgan had been looking for. She was pretty without being vain, intelligent without needing to have the last word. They attended parties, occasionally went to church together, and created a small circle of friends. She had moved to Pueblo from Omaha a couple of months before Morgan, found work in a bank and lived in a boarding house for women. They met when he visited the bank to open an account. That evening he invited her for dinner at the Nugget Inn, a favorite eating place for locals. What might have been a promising future for the two ended when she returned to Omaha to care for her ailing mother. She never returned to Pueblo.

Morgan's reverie was jolted hard by the sound of a loud commotion. A dogfight had started and three men were trying to break it up.

Making his way through the crowd to check on the ruckus, Morgan was suddenly shoved hard from behind and almost knocked to the ground. Regaining his balance, he turned quickly and faced Robertson and the two strangers. Before Morgan could grasp what was happening, Robertson struck Morgan hard on the jaw. As Morgan hit the ground, the two baboons began kicking him in the ribs and groin. Morgan grabbed one of the attacker's legs, twisted it hard and slammed his boot into the stomach of the surprised thug. The other man was caught off balance and fell in a heap on top of his buddy. Robertson jockeyed in position to use a board he found lying nearby. Seeing a good opening, Robertson raised the board above his head and started to swing.

A shotgun blast split the air and Robertson froze.

"That'll do!" Porter shouted. "I got another barrel full of shot, if any of you jaybirds want it. Now, find your horses and get out of town before I march you down to the jailhouse."

Robertson addressed the two strangers. "Go on. Git to work. You've got plenty of it to do."

Before leaving, one of the men glared menacingly at

Morgan and the other at Porter. Robertson turned and began walking in the direction of Porter's house.

"If you're going to be looking to see Lorna, Al, you can forget it. She told me when she left the schoolyard that she wanted both you and Morgan to keep away from her."

Robertson changed direction and called over his shoulder to Morgan. "I'll be seein' you again, city slicker. And when I do it'll be a different story."

Morgan took a few steps toward Robertson before Porter stepped in front of him. "What I said was meant for everyone. That includes you."

Chapter Twelve

After talking with Amos Porter for a few minutes and getting Porter's promise to convey an apology to Lorna, Morgan left town for the Rocking Ewe. He thought better of following the road, supposing some back-shooter could be waiting for him, so he moved a mile or so to the north and followed a seldom-used trail through the hilly countryside. Finding fresh wagon wheel tracks on the overgrown trail was a surprise.

He was disappointed with the way the day had gone, and disappointed in the role he played in not making it better. His job was to assure the community it would be protected from harm and that Seth Ruddell's troubles had nothing to do with them or their safety. So much for that, he thought.

He concluded being an investigator in a city was much

easier than in the country. His city jobs had been mostly cut and dried: mining companies needing security, finding store clerks who embezzle, helping politicians find skeletons in their opponents' closets, running background checks on persons involved in large financial deals, and working with lawyers on cases requiring information not readily available through regular channels.

But he was starting to appreciate the difference his efforts could make if he kept a cool head and grew some thicker skin.

Morgan slowed the gelding to listen more closely to what sounded like moaning in the underbrush. He dismounted, pulled his Colt from its holster and walked cautiously toward the sound. Parting a large clump of bushes, Morgan found the shaking form of a man, hands tied behind his back, feet bound together, and bleeding from a large gash in the back of his skull. Morgan gently rolled the man onto his back.

It was Ben Clark!

"Ben! What in thunder's going on? What happened?"

"They got Millie an' the wagon. Two men. Saw 'em at the school today. I done all I could to stop 'em, but I got hit real hard. That was the last I knew 'til I come to here in the bushes all trussed up"

Morgan quickly released Clark's hands and feet, and tied his bandanna tightly around Clark's head to cover the wound.

"What did the men say?" Morgan asked.

"Didn't say a word. They was just laughin' an' hootin' an' carryin' on like they was crazy. The more Millie screamed, the more they laughed. Help me up, Clemet. I gotta go find her." Clark tried to get to his feet but fell backward into the brush.

"Whoa, son, steady there. That's a big hurt you got on the back of your head. You need to take it easy."

"Got no time to take it easy. Millie's out there, who knows where? Them two was loco crazy, an' smellin' like whiskey. We gotta find her!"

Morgan had to make a tough call. The longer he waited to go after the skunks, the farther away they would be. Clark was in no condition to go on a chase; he needed medical attention. Leaving him alone in the hills wouldn't be smart. Morgan decided they'd ride double and head for the Rocking Ewe.

The gelding balked some as Morgan helped Clark into the saddle and climbed on behind, but he settled as Morgan set his gait at a walk and little by little increased the cadence to a trot, then a canter, and finally pushed him to a full gallop. For the last mile, the horse seemed as eager to get home as his two riders.

Reaching the ranch house, Morgan quickly helped Clark inside and laid him on the sofa. From the bedroom, Ruddell, hearing Morgan getting Clark settled, shook himself awake and hobbled into the parlor. Learning of Millie's abduction alarmed and distressed Ruddell. Tears filled his eyes.

"Help me into my riding clothes," Ruddell demanded. "And saddle my horse. We've got to get out there and find her while she's still alive."

"Seth, you can't ride!" Morgan was quickly considering all possibilities. "You're the one who'll be dead if you try a stunt like that. Let's sit down and try to figure out why this happened. Nothing can be done until morning. We can't track the wagon in the dark, my horse is worn out, and Ben needs to be tended."

Clark had fallen asleep on the sofa so Morgan and Ruddell sat at the kitchen table searching for an answer as to why Millie was taken. The most logical conclusion was simple: The wagon was stolen for the supplies, as well as rustling the horses. However, the more they talked, the more unreasonable that seemed as a motive. What would two drifters do with a wagonload of flour, sugar, beans, and dog food? Beyond that, why would they even want a wagon? Of course the Clydesdales could be sold for cash but everyone for miles around would recognize the Rocking Ewe brand and know the horses were stolen. No, there had to be a better reason. They couldn't let themselves believe the worse-case scenario; that two drunken drifters had nabbed Millie just because she was there for the taking. After all, these galoots didn't know who she was, and even if they did there was nothing to gain by kidnapping her. They were undoubtedly too stupid to know how to demand ransom for her return.

But what about their connection with Robertson? He was seen with the two men at the festival and they were a part of the attempted gang-beating of Morgan. Morgan had shrugged off that skirmish as Robertson's jealousy over Lorna Porter. However, maybe there was more to it—something more sinister. For lack of a better place to start, Morgan chose to believe Robertson had a hand in this crime.

Out on the range, crew boss Harry Samuels was doing his best to keep spirits high and bellies full, but the uncertainty as to what might happen next cast a cloud over the usually free-spirited comrades. Swift Eagle and the Navajos had tracked and recovered thirty-seven of the stampeded rams. Leaving one Navajo on the range to continue the search, Swift Eagle and the others returned to the flock. Finding the rams should have been a bright spot, but to a few herders this just meant more sheep to tend.

Long days and tense hours had taken their toll on two members of the crew and they lit out as soon as the Navajos returned. Samuels had pleaded with them not to go, even taking it on himself to offer bonuses for staying, but they didn't take the deal.

Then something else unexpected happened to further deplete the workforce. Two days earlier Robertson rode into the compound and spent a great deal of time talking one-to-one with the herders on duty, working around the wide perimeter of the contained flock. Samuels observed this strange activity and confronted Robertson, who explained he was receiving a shipment of two-hundred head of cattle he hadn't expected to arrive until spring and needed some wranglers. All of Robertson's regulars had gone to Mexico for the winter so he was looking to do a quick hire.

Samuels had some choice words to share with Robertson before ordering him off the land, but the damage was done. As Robertson galloped away toward the Alawanda, two Rocking Ewe men were riding alongside.

Morgan greeted dawn the next morning with no better plan of action than when he met the darkness the night before. Neither he nor Ruddell were able to sleep. Clark was quiet for most of the night, except for an occasional moan every hour when Morgan applied horse liniment to Clark's wound.

Ruddell insisted that he try to get on his horse and help search for Millie until Morgan persuaded him to stay at the house in case contact was made. Before leaving, Morgan instructed Clark to take a report to Harry Samuels as soon as Clark felt he could ride. He was to tell Samuels everything, but Samuels was not to tell the men. They had to know, however, the supply wagon would be late in coming and they needed to stretch their rations for a few more days.

Leaving the ranch, Morgan was in another quandary. His first thought was to find the wagon tracks and chase after the thieves as quickly as possible. Finding Millie unharmed was his major concern. But was that the best tactic? To this point, only Clark and Ruddell knew what was going on. If Morgan acted on emotion—and was killed—it would be days before anyone would know about the problem, making the chance of finding Millie highly unlikely. Going into Red Mountain seemed to be the better option. Once there he could try to raise a posse. But, without a sheriff, could there even be a legal posse? Not that it mattered at this point, but a legally sworn body of men is what separates law-abiders from vigilantes.

Morgan headed for Red Mountain.

The day after Al Robertson lured away two of the Rocking Ewe crew, a violent thunderstorm moved down from the mountains and into the valley where the flock was being held. It didn't last long, but the rain was heavy. Brilliant lightning in streaks of white and blue jumped like a rattler's tongue from the black clouds.

Simon Gray Wolf, the Navajo tracker left behind to search for more stampeded rams, took shelter in a thicket of trees. His dog, trying to find even more dense cover, burrowed into the middle of a stand of tall grass, only to run out quickly, barking excitedly. Gray Wolf waded through the waist-high foliage until his foot hit an object. Parting the grass for a better look, he found the bodies of two men he immediately recognized as herdsmen for the Rocking Ewe. Both had been shot in the back.

Clemet Morgan needed help. Too many bad things were happening too quickly to handle alone. He could send one of the herders to Santa Fe to get help from the territorial marshal; but that would take days, with no assurance any help would be available. Harold Gainer was the only person in the region with the expertise to send telegrams and Harold was dead. People in and around Red Mountain were spooked by the bits of information they had about the killings. The school board met at the end of Harvest Festival and decided to suspend school until the area was safe. They would rather have their children uneducated than harmed.

The kidnapping of Millie Ruddell would send another shudder through the community, escalating the level of fear even higher. Amos Porter could be counted on to help, and probably John Bundy. But beyond those two, prospects were grim. Pulling herders in from the range would leave the sheep at the mercy of predatory animals and human marauders.

Clearly, the many unknown factors would present a big challenge to any plan Morgan might devise.

Clark left the ranch house mid-afternoon, some eight hours after Morgan headed for Red Mountain. Before he could reach the holding area Clark became ill from his wounded skull and had to stop for the night. Feeling better by morning, he and Simon Gray Wolf arrived at the herd within ten minutes of each other, both eager to report to Samuels the misdeeds of the past two days.

Clark wanted to tell his story and head back to join the search for Millie. Gray Wolf located Swift Eagle, hoping he could interpret the tragedy of finding two of the Rocking

Ewe herders murdered. The Navajos reached Samuels just as Clark was finishing his account. Samuels was full of questions for Clark but he didn't get to ask them as Swift Eagle excitedly broke into the conversation.

"Gray Wolf find two men dead," he related. "Ones Robertson took to work on ranch. Robertson not there—just two men, shot in back."

"What in the name of Jupiter's goin' on?" Samuels asked. "Men gittin' killed; girls bein' kidnapped. Just don't make a lick a' sense."

Samuels looked at Clark. "Did Morgan tell you what we're supposed to do?"

"No, only that the supply wagon'll be late and don't tell the men about Millie."

"I ain't gonna tell the men 'bout these killin's neither," Samuels said. "We're down to the nubbins as is. If this gits 'round, everone'll skedaddle."

Getting to Red Mountain, Morgan went directly to Amos Porter's livery stable, only to find the door padlocked. Momentarily confused, Morgan sat on the edge of a horse trough in front of the barn. He was exhausted, not unlike his first day in Red Mountain when he found sleep in the open barn which was now locked. Porter had told Morgan that from the day he bought the livery and blacksmith business, he had never locked the door. "Folks are really honest in this neck of the woods," he said with great pride. "If the time comes I need to lock the door, I'll know that's the day I should be thinking about moving on."

Morgan slowly climbed into the saddle for the ride to Porter's house. Realizing how tired the gelding was, he dismounted, loosened the saddle cinch, led the horse to the trough and tied the reins to a hitching post. He would walk to find Porter.

Nearing the house, he saw Lorna sitting on the porch peeling apples. She was so deep in thought that Morgan was almost to the front gate before she looked up. She was startled to see him.

"What are you doing back in town? Or, did you even leave?"

There was irritation in her voice.

"Yeah, I left. There's a problem I need to talk over with Amos. Is he home?"

"No, he's out trying to persuade a few men to join the city council. He'll be along. Ma and the boys are at the store helping Nell do the inventory. I'm here to make supper. However, speaking of a problem, I've got one of my own. Since you're a big part of it, why don't we have a little discussion?"

Lorna didn't wait for Morgan to respond before continuing.

"What kind of stubborn mule are you? The regular kind or one that walks on his hind legs thinking he's a man? Given the choice of which I'd rather be with, I'll take the regular variety. But I see you standing there on your hind legs."

"Are you talking about the auction?"

"You're really smart for a mule," Lorna shot back.

"Yes, the auction. And the face-off with Al Robertson. And almost getting your stubborn mule head split open if Pa hadn't stepped in."

"I see you're too mad at me to talk. You've got a right to be. I *was* acting like a mule, and I'm sorry. Please ask Amos to meet me at the livery, if I don't see him along the way. Tell him it's about Millie Ruddell."

"Millie? What about Millie? Did something happen to her?"

"Yes, something terrible. She's been kidnapped."

Lorna stood quickly to her feet, spilling the bowl of apples.

"Why would anyone kidnap Millie? When did it happen?"

"Yesterday. She and Ben Clark were driving the supply wagon back to the Rocking Ewe when those two crackers who were with Robertson at the festival jumped them. They beat Ben up and left him to die, then made off with Millie and the wagon. Seth was fit to be tied and wanted to take out after them, broken bones and all. I convinced him he needed to stay at the ranch in case the kidnappers tried to make contact. But he didn't like it."

"You don't think Al had anything to do with this, do you?"

"Can't rule anyone out. You know him better than most. Is he someone I should be looking at?"

"I don't know. This is so confusing. Al was a nice man and seemed to love his wife and kids very much. They would always be in church together, and he volunteered to help whenever there was a need. I'll have to admit, I did see quite a change in Al after Wanda died. He told me once, right after her death, that he felt like a failure."

"How so?"

"Her family didn't think Al was good enough for Wanda. Even though he'd bought that little ranch, they wanted her to wait for a better offer. When she went against them and married Al, he promised her that someday he'd have the biggest spread in this part of New Mexico. He wanted to show her—and her family—he could be as successful as any man."

"Is that why he's pushing Seth so hard to sell?"

"I suspect that's part of it. The irony is, even if Seth agreed to sell, there's no way Al could afford to buy. I always thought it was just a game the two played."

"Could be. But remember the last meeting Al had with Seth? Al said he had a backer who was going to pull out if a deal wasn't put together quick."

"I do remember," Lorna said. "That's when I saw a side of Al I hadn't known. He was really scary. This whole thing is scary. Poor Millie. We have to find her. We have to get her back."

"And we will. But we need to have a plan to make sure we do it right. No matter how much we want to tear out after the goons who have her, we've got to think it through."

Both were quiet for a minute or two. Lorna collected the apples that had dropped and Morgan held the bowl for her to put them in, wiping away the dust from the ones that had been peeled. Her hand touched his as she reached to take the bowl, and for a brief moment Morgan was somewhere else in his mind; a place peaceful and worry-free, a place quiet and cool and filled with promise, a place he had dreamed of so many nights—so many lonely nights. He longed to take this beautiful woman in his arms, to assure her that everything would be all right, that he was there for her and would always be there for her.

"Hey, Clemet! I thought that was your gelding tied up at the livery."

The booming voice of Porter jerked Morgan back to reality.

"What brings you to town? If you want to buy Lorna's picnic basket from me I can make you a good price."

Porter, Mayor of Red Mountain, New Mexico, sat and listened in disbelief as Morgan recounted the story of Millie's abduction. His tranquil little center of commerce for farmers and ranchers was suddenly in the eye of a hurricane, bringing with it robbery, murder, and now, kidnapping.

Porter's meetings with four prospective council members had not been fruitful. A fog bank of fear was engulfing the community and nobody seemed willing to step forward. Porter was tired and frustrated to the point of resigning. If he couldn't find anyone who cared enough about Red Mountain to help govern it, why should he?

"Because you *do* care," Lorna insisted. "You stepped into a job that nobody wanted and you've kept this community alive and growing. As bad as things are now, they'll get better. And the reason they'll get better is because of you."

"I love you for saying that, darling. But I'm just one man," Porter said with a deep sigh. "I'm a mayor without a town council. Red Mountain is a town without a sheriff. And the people I promised to protect are sleeping with guns under their pillows."

"Amos," Morgan said quietly, "Seth may not like it much, but I'll be your sheriff until you find someone to take the job."

Morgan declined Lorna's supper invitation. Every part of his body was telling him to stay, but his mind won the struggle. So many things needed to be done and there was so little time to do them. His thoughts and prayers were with Millie and her safekeeping. What a devastating loss it would be to Seth if she was killed. They were everything to each other.

Before leaving, Porter gave Morgan the oath of office, making him the official sheriff of Red Mountain. A badge similar to the one worn by Gainer the day he was shot was handed to Morgan. He decided the star would stay in his pocket most of the time.

As he rounded the corner leading to the livery stable Morgan saw a horse tied next to his at the hitching post. He cautiously moved toward the barn, resting his palm on the handle of his Colt. When he was a few yards from the water trough he recognized the second horse.

"Jamison!" Morgan said in a soft shout. "Jamison Jakes, where are you?"

"I'm back here, Clem. Be right there." Within seconds, Jakes, Morgan's partner from Pueblo, appeared from behind the barn.

"I was lookin' for a way into the barn to get some feed for my horse."

"What in creation are you doing here?" Morgan asked, smiling broadly.

"Got a telegram from Sheriff Gainer sayin' you could use some help, so I scurried down here fast as I could."

Jakes opened his saddlebag, pulled out the telegram and handed it to Morgan.

Mister Jakes STOP I know he would say otherwise but I got a feeling that your partner will need your help before long STOP If there is a way you can come to Red Mountain that would be real good STOP I will try to keep him out of trouble until you arrive STOP Sheriff Harold Gainer

The telegram was dated the morning of the day Gainer was murdered.

"I tried to send an answer back sayin' I'd be comin' but the telegraph man in Pueblo said the key was closed on this end and he couldn't get through."

"What about Maryalice and the baby," Morgan wanted to know. "I thought you needed to stay close to home."

"I thought that way too, but her thought was different. She reminded me of the nervous wreck I was when Daniel was born. She all but begged me to get down here out of her way. She's got ladies from the church lookin' in on her around the clock and carin' for Daniel. Besides, we may have this job all done before it's her time to deliver."

The moon was full and marked the road as Morgan and Jakes made their way to the Rocking Ewe. Morgan's account of all that happened—from the day he shot Chad Barton until Millie's kidnapping—drew whistles and grunts from Jakes. With each progressive event, the task of finding a solution to the problems confronting them became more daunting. The loss of Ruddell's rams was now overshadowed by the murders of Jed Nooley and Harold Gainer and Millie's kidnapping. Unknown to Morgan and Jakes at the time they were heading for the ranch, two other men had been senselessly killed.

Chapter Thirteen

Seth Ruddell and Ben Clark were anxiously awaiting Morgan's return from Red Mountain, with the hope he would have news of Millie. They kept each other company through the long hours by telling stories of times remembered, when Millie and Clark were children. While Ruddell and Clark felt the same angry passion to get out into the countryside to look for Millie, they agreed that would be futile. Morgan was the man in charge, the one experienced in dealing with lawlessness and looking for lawbreakers. If anyone could find Millie, it would be Morgan.

As the night crept, Clark shared with Ruddell his fondness for Millie and confessed she was the reason he had returned to Red Mountain: to discover if the strong feelings he had for her as kid were still there and, if so, to court her. Should the relationship develop to the point of discussing marriage, Clark intended to ask Ruddell's permission to marry his granddaughter.

However, current circumstances compelled Clark to speak his mind now. He wanted Ruddell to know those strong feelings *were* still there. Even stronger. So strong and sure was his love for Millie, he wanted Ruddell's permission now to ask Millie to be his wife.

Clark's confession had a peaceful, calming effect on the old man. Since the altercation in Bartonville left Ruddell all but helpless, he had been concerned about who would be there for Millie if he died. Ruddell had always liked Clark, first as a youngster and now as a man. He motioned Clark to come to his chair. Ruddell held Clark's hand tightly and, without saying a word, both bowed their heads in silent prayer.

When Morgan and Jakes got within shouting distance of the house and saw lamps still lit, Morgan shouted, "Hello, the house! Morgan coming in!" Almost immediately the front door opened and Clark stepped onto the porch, lamp in hand.

Seeing in the dim, flickering light there was a second rider, Clark yelled excitedly, "Is that Millie with you? Did you find her?"

"Sorry, Ben," Morgan replied. "It's not Millie. But it is someone who'll help us find her."

By the time Morgan and Jakes dismounted and hitched their horses to the rail, Ruddell had managed to get himself to the door. Realizing Millie was not with Morgan, his body sagged against the doorframe.

During the next hour, discussion centered on Clark's telling of the two herdsmen being killed and Morgan telling Ruddell and Clark about what had taken place in Red Mountain.

Ruddell was okay with Morgan filling in as sheriff. Since it was obvious that everything going sour was connected to Morgan's investigation already underway on the ranch, he was the logical person to act as sheriff. Ruddell found Jakes' arrival serendipitous and a great boost to his confidence that Millie would be found—especially after learning Jakes had years of experience as a bounty hunter and could track almost as good as an Indian. Since Jakes was a stranger, he would have freedom of movement through the region without drawing suspicion.

The night proved restless for all. Nonetheless, the quiet time gave an opportunity for each man to silently reflect on his life—on things that mattered most.

Millie filled the thoughts of Ruddell and Clark, but for different reasons. She was all Ruddell had left in life. If he lost her, he would have no one. Clark was hoping for a life with Millie; but now he was in a world of hurt and sorrow, wishing he'd been forthright in telling her as soon as he returned to Red Mountain he was there because of her.

Jakes thought of home and Maryalice, their son Daniel, and the new baby, nearly born, who might have arrived by now. Morgan drifted into sleep finding rest in the arms of Lorna Porter.

When dawn arrived, the strategy they developed was simple, but thorough. Ruddell would stay at the house and wait for contact from the kidnappers, Clark would return to the herd with a report for Samuels that the supply delivery would be delayed even longer, and the scout-savvy Jakes would track the wagon from the point of Millie's abduction. Morgan, as sheriff, would go for a showdown with Robertson at the Alawanda.

Arriving at the herd, Clark was immediately aware that something was amiss. There were no outriders holding the sheep in check. Some of the dogs were on duty, but they seemed worn out. As he neared the shack serving as headquarters for the herdsmen, he heard loud voices arguing and swearing. A small crowd of men stood in a semicircle with Samuels in front, speaking firmly. Swift Eagle and the Navajos were not in the group.

"I just don't git it!" Samuels was saying. "We got a job to do, a job we all signed on fer. If you pull out now it'll be the ruination of Seth. If you can deal with that fer the rest a' your worthless lives, then git on outta here!"

"We don't wanna be killed where we stand," Joe Nixon, one of the older herders said. "Better to live with shame than die fightin' someone else's battle. Them two boys what got killed would be alive today if this here feud hadn't been goin' on."

Samuels was ready to shoot back a response, but stopped when Clark rode in.

"Hey Ben! Glad you're back!" Samuels said. "These

chicken bellies are 'bout to fly the coop. We're gonna need you. All we got left workin' out here now is Swift Eagle and his braves, an' they can't do it all."

"Have you told them about Millie?" Clark asked. "Since they're all pullin' out anyway, no need to keep that from 'em."

Samuels agreed, and Clark spared no detail in relating the latest black cloud hanging over the Rocking Ewe and Seth Ruddell. At the end of his monologue Clark pleaded with the men to stay on, at least until Millie was found.

Morgan rode with Jakes to the spot where the drunken thugs had jumped the wagon. A clear trail of tracks led off to the northeast. With a wave of his hand, Jakes rode in that direction. The two partners agreed on the way to the abduction site that caution would be key in this part of the investigation. The main purpose was to make sure Millie was unharmed and assess the possibility of a rescue. Jakes had learned a lesson from a seasoned bounty hunter many years before. The law has two aspects: bad guys get caught and then get a fair trial. This had become Jakes' not-to-be questioned guiding rule.

The wagon trail was not difficult to follow. There was no attempt on the part of the thieves to cover their tracks. In fact, it looked as though they were making it easy for someone to find them. This alone sounded an alarm in Jakes' head, making him ride deeper into the woods while still keeping an eye on the trail. Being ambushed would not help matters. It was obvious the direction of the wagon hadn't changed so Jakes stayed pointed in a northeasterly direction, moving at a slow but steady pace.

It was also clear to Jakes the wagon had kept moving. There was no sign of a campsite and, best of all, he saw nothing to suggest that anything had happened to Millie. The urge for Jakes to move faster was constantly there and had to be kept in check.

When the light became too dim to follow the trail, Jakes prepared to stop for the night. He knew a fire wasn't possible, but his bedroll held two large wool blankets and his saddlebags were full of venison jerky and biscuits. This was a life he thought he had given up when he joined Morgan's detective agency—a life of cold nights sleeping on the ground, eating dried food, and waiting for mornings that never seem to come. What goes around comes around, he concluded, making himself as comfortable as possible.

While Jakes was tracking the wagon and Clark was reporting to Samuels, Morgan cautiously approached Robertson's Alawanda ranch. Staying under cover of a large grove of cottonwoods surrounding the house and using a single-eye telescope, he studied the building from every side. There was no activity in the yard and, as best he could see through the windows, no movement inside.

Morgan tied the gelding's reins to a tree, removed his Winchester from its scabbard and moved in a crouched position stealthily toward the barn. Inside the barn, Morgan's instincts kicked in when he found a horse put away wet and shivering in the afternoon coolness. He covered the animal with a blanket. If the horse belonged to Robertson, why didn't he take time to put him away properly? If not Robertson, then who was the person? And where was he, if not in the house?

Knowing he needed a closer look through the windows, Morgan quickly removed his spurs and hat and quietly positioned himself under a window on the back side of the house. Slithering into an upright position at the side of the window Morgan peered inside. A man was sitting at the kitchen table, his hands covering his head. Morgan realized from the jerky motion of the man's shoulders he was crying.

Using the element of surprise, Morgan kicked open the door and aimed his rifle at the startled man jumping to his feet. It was Tommy Hunt, Robertson's brother-in-law! Holding both hands high above his head, the look on the boy's face reflected both fear and anguish.

"Use the thumb and one finger of your left hand, lift your revolver by its handle, drop it on the floor and move away from it," Morgan demanded. "Then sit down before you fall down. You're as white as a snow bank."

After getting rid of his gun, Hunt slumped heavily into a chair, put his head in his hands and began to cry again.

"Get a grip on yourself, boy, and tell me what in God's green earth is going on."

"They got Millie. They got Millie, an' they's gonna kill her if her grandpa don't sell his ranch to Al."

"Where are they holding her?"

"Somewhere up 'round Bartonville. Al come into town where I been stayin' with my folks after I brought his girls up. He was lookin' for me so's I could take word they got Millie. They'll trade her for the deed to the Rockin' Ewe."

"So that's his dirty game, is it? Robertson knew he'd never get the Rocking Ewe legally so he's stooped to kidnapping."

"He don't call it kidnappin', he calls it persuasion, or somethin' like that. He plans to pay Seth for the land, so he says it ain't like stealin'."

"What were you told to do? When is Robertson expecting an answer?"

"I gotta talk with Seth. No one else. Since Al killed Harold Gainer he knows there ain't no law 'round for Seth to go runnin' to. He give me three days to come back with the answer."

There it was. Morgan's gut feeling that either Lester Hobson or Hunt had murdered the sheriff flew out the window. Robertson was the killer! And killing one man in cold blood made it even easier for Robertson to slaughter the two Rocking Ewe men to get what he was after. A man can be hanged only once, no matter how many he's murdered.

"Come on!" Morgan said, roughly pulling the boy to his feet. "We're going to the Rocking Ewe and give Seth your message. He needs to know that Millie's still alive."

Jamison Jakes finished his cold supper and wrapped himself in the two blankets, hoping for sleep. He was close to dozing off when he heard his horse whinny. Startled, he grabbed his Colt from under the saddle he was using as a headrest, instinctively rolled to his right, and sprang to his feet.

In the dim light of a half moon, Jakes could make out the forms of two large horses, standing quietly next to his mare. He moved slowly toward them, speaking in a soft, reassuring voice.

Clydesdales! Jakes ran his hands along the side of one of these gentle giants, moving toward its flank to read the brand. As he suspected, these draft horses were the ones pulling the Rocking Ewe wagon when Millie was nabbed.

Jakes decided not to tie or hobble the horses. If they were still in camp at daybreak, he would give it more thought; if not, he would assume they were making their way back to the ranch on their own. His main goal for morning would be to locate Millie and the wagon.

It was well after dark when Morgan and Hunt arrived at Ruddell's house. As always, Morgan shouted a greeting to alert Ruddell that riders were coming in. However, unlike the other times, there was no response from the house. Morgan shouted a second time. Still no response. After a third try, Morgan heard the clanging of metal against metal coming from the barn and hurried to check the noise.

Entering the darkened barn, Morgan saw movement in the stable area. He called Seth's name, getting a muffled reply. Morgan grabbed a kerosene lantern from the hook inside the barn's entry, found a box of matches on the shelf above the hook and lit the lantern. In the flickering light, Morgan saw the slumped form of Ruddell on the barn floor, his saddled horse standing over him, his crutches leaning against a paddock gate.

"What's going on, Seth? Why in the world are you out here?"

"I just couldn't sit in the house doing nothing while my Millie's only God-knows-where . . ." Ruddell's voice became weaker and finally lost all sound, although his lips continued to move. Morgan sized up the situation. Ruddell had tried to get on his horse and had fallen in the attempt. There were no signs of blood or other injuries. The old man had just keeled over from fatigue.

Using a large wooden wheelbarrow, Morgan and Hunt managed to get Ruddell back into the house and onto his bed.

"Let's let him sleep for as long as it takes him to get back his senses," Morgan said. "Until then, boy, you tell me everything you know about what's going on. And I mean *everything.*"

With the help of Swift Eagle, Samuels and Clark were able to convince what was left of the Rocking Ewe crew to stay on. The afternoon before Clark arrived with the disturbing news about Millie, Swift Eagle sent two of the Navajos out to look for signs of anyone prowling around the herd. Neither had found anything suspicious. These reports seemed to settle the nerves of the men somewhat, but most were still jittery. One more unexpected bad circumstance, Samuels knew, might cause the whole group to bolt.

Samuels found himself wondering how things would be different if the entire crew had the gumption of Clark or the loyalty of Swift Eagle and the Navajos. Being out here doing a job was what the men were hired to do. But all they expected when they signed on was to be fed every day and get paid a good wage at the end of the month. This is the way it had always been. Until now.

It started falling apart, the other men concluded, when Morgan arrived. Everything had been calm to the point of boredom before then. Boredom is good for a sheep-herder; he knows what to expect and when to expect it. During times of boredom rams aren't stolen, co-workers and friends aren't murdered, and young girls aren't kidnapped.

Jamison Jakes awoke with a start. To what must have been a twig breaking under the hoof of one of the horses, he reacted as though an attack was in the making. His early years in the Confederate Army, his somewhat wasted life as a drifter, and his stint as a bounty hunter all fed into his alertness to unusual sounds.

This time he guessed right. The Clydesdales stood next to Jakes' mare, pawing the ground and wondering when the day's work would begin. Jakes wished he knew.

Morgan kept Hunt awake long enough to get a feel for what was happening. Through bouts of crying and sniffling,

Hunt confessed that until the killings started, he was willing to help Robertson get ownership of the Rocking Ewe. He hadn't counted on anyone getting physically harmed, let alone murdered.

Hunt had recruited Jed Nooley with a wad of Robertson's cash, and Nooley was to bring Hobson into the gang as well. When Hobson refused and threatened to tell Ruddell what was going on, Nooley drew down on Hobson; but Hobson was a blink faster and plugged Nooley first. Hunt witnessed the shootout and warned Hobson if he spilled his guts to anyone, Robertson would have him killed.

After hearing this, Morgan knew Hobson wasn't the cold-blooded murderer he'd figured him to be; rather, just a scared man running from trouble, trying to stay alive.

Hunt also opened up about the message from Robertson he was to deliver to Ruddell. If Ruddell signed the Rocking Ewe over to Robertson, Millie would be returned unharmed. The exchange of Millie for the deed would be made at the jailhouse. Robertson would have a bunch of men riding with him to ensure there would be no foul–ups. To make it legal and proper, Amos Porter, as mayor, would witness Ruddell's signature and give Robertson a receipt for payment of the land, pegged at fifty cents an acre.

Morgan wanted to believe everything Hunt told him was true. If so, they could be certain of Millie's safe return. With only a handful of men willing to go up against Robertson's large band of scurvy misfits, Morgan felt the only option for getting Millie returned unharmed was to agree to Robertson's terms.

Knowing that tomorrow would come quickly and be a full day, Morgan took the boy to the barn. To make certain Hunt would still be there in the morning, Morgan tied him hand and foot in the windowless tack room and padlocked the door. Morgan checked on Ruddell, who was sleeping soundly, then stretched out on the sofa and waited for dawn.

Chapter Fourteen

Out on the range, the herdsmen had reconciled their differences with Harry Samuels and were back into a steady routine; nonetheless, a few were grumbling about growing tired of rationing their food. Although two fires were going constantly, with large haunches of mutton always available, the men were hungry for fruit and vegetables. And adding to their concerns, the coffee stash was almost depleted.

Being familiar with the procedure for buying supplies, Ben Clark was assigned to go to town and replace everything that was on the supply wagon when it was stolen. Samuels told him to head for the ranch house. If the horses and wagon hadn't been found, he was to borrow a team and wagon from Porter's livery, then hightail it back. As before, Clark would ride as far as possible before dark, camp for a few hours, then move on when there was enough light to see the trail.

The pounding of his horse's hooves kept cadence with the pounding of his heart as Clark prayed for Millie's safe return.

Hard as he tried, Jamison Jakes couldn't convince the Clydesdales to keep moving toward home. The branch he used as a willow switch on their hindquarters was met with little more than tail flicks. After breaking camp and continuing to follow the wagon trail, the Clydesdales trotted behind Jakes' mare as if she'd invited them to come along. This is great, Jakes thought. How do you sneak up on kidnappers—or anyone—with two tons of horseflesh trotting in your shadow?

By staying hidden in the trees bordering the trail, Jakes almost missed the smoke from a chimney, rising through the early morning fog and swirling in the breeze. Then there it was: A large log cabin in the middle of a clearing. To one side of the cabin, Jakes made out the shape of a wagon. Directly in front were a dozen hobbled horses.

Fearing the Clydesdales would want to visit the small herd, Jakes took the two—along with his mare—deeper into the forest and tied them to trees. Then, moving as close to the cabin as he felt comfortable doing, he waited with his telescope for something to happen.

It was not a long wait.

A side door opened. A girl with two men, one on each side, gripping her elbows, walked quickly toward the outhouse. Once there, the men stood guard while the girl closed the door. By all accounting, the girl had to be Millie Ruddell.

Five minutes after the trio reentered the cabin, the front door opened. A short, heavyset man came into the yard, grabbed a saddle and blanket from a tree limb where they were hanging, threw them on the back of a horse, cinched the saddle tightly, and mounted. When the horse refused to move, despite hard kicks to her ribs, the fat man swore loudly at the animal. Responding to the commotion, another man came out, summed up the situation, and laughed heartily.

"You dumb cracker," the second man yelled to the one on the horse. "If you take off that hobble, the horse'll prob'ly move!"

Jakes chuckled softly. An outlaw this stupid can be one of two things: Either very easy to get a jump on or very dangerous to confront. Jakes decided to see which was true for this dimwit.

Moving quickly to where the mare and Clydesdales were tied, Jakes mounted his horse and struck out in the direction the man had taken. The Clydesdales strained at their ropes attempting to follow before settling down. Jakes would stay in the trees—away from the trail—until he was ahead of the rider and then surprise the man before he had a chance to react.

Some plans work, some don't. To Jakes' relief, this plan worked. When he stepped onto the trail from his hiding place, his Winchester leveled at the man's large belly,

Jakes quickly discovered the category of dimwit he was dealing with.

"Don't shoot me, mister," the man begged. "I got some money. It ain't much but you can have it. Your can have my horse too. Just please don't kill me!"

"I don't want your money, or you horse. And whether or not I kill you depends on how you answer my questions."

Clemet Morgan was up well before dawn. Checking on Ruddell after starting to brew a pot of coffee, he found the old man awake, responsive, and anxious to know if there was news of Millie. Morgan placed two large goose-down pillows behind Ruddell's back, getting him into a sitting position against the headboard. Morgan assured him there was news, but first Morgan needed something from the barn.

Tommy Hunt twitched when Morgan unlocked and opened the tack room door, but continued his onerous snoring until Morgan lightly kicked Hunt's rear with the toe of his boot.

"Wake up!" Morgan demanded. "We've got a lot to do, and little time to do it."

Ruddell's face was a mask of surprised confusion when Morgan brought Hunt into the bedroom with his hands bound tightly in front of him. Ruddell's gray, shaggy mane tilted to one side, then the other, before his eyes fixed squarely on Hunt, standing with his head down, looking like a kid about to get a whacking.

"Tommy's got something to tell you, Seth," Morgan said, glaring at Hunt. "It's not a pretty story. In fact, it's downright ugly."

Staring at the floor from start to finish, Hunt retold the story of Al Robertson's two-year attempt to obtain the Rocking Ewe. Subtle means—like stealing rams—proved to take too long. Working from inside the herding crew did nothing, except get Jed Nooley killed by his partner, Lester Hobson. The murder of Harold Gainer to eliminate any semblance of law in Red Mountain hadn't worked like Robertson had hoped. And killing the two herdsmen in cold blood—trying to scare off the others—backfired.

Robertson's original desire of getting ownership of the Rocking Ewe to prove himself to Wanda's family had slowly evolved into crazed, demonic greed. The kidnapping of Millie and demanding the deed to the Rocking Ewe as ransom was the last desperate act of a desperate man bent on satisfying this greed.

For Ruddell, the decision was easy. He had put much of his life into making the Rocking Ewe the thriving enterprise it had become. His son and daughter-in-law had been swept to their deaths trying to be there with him. Starting with the thousand acres on which he once raised cattle, he pastured five hundred sheep. By braving hot, searing summers and freezing winters, he kept his small herd alive and growing until the Rocking Ewe had expanded to a four-thousand-acre spread and was finally making a good profit. While befriending neighbors, Navajos, townspeople, and strangers, he had offended no one.

No one, that is, until Robertson began his campaign to run Ruddell out of business, and out of town.

Nothing was worth more than Millie's life—absolutely nothing—Ruddell concluded. If he had to sacrifice the Rocking Ewe to get her back safely, he would sign over the deed in a heartbeat.

Morgan knew Ruddell would do everything for Millie, but thought some options were still open. After all, Robertson and his gang had no idea Hunt had found a conscience and confessed, not just to his own crimes but Robertson's as well. Nor did he know that Red Mountain had a new—though temporary—sheriff. What if Hunt returned to Bartonville, reported to Robertson that all had gone smoothly, and Ruddell had agreed to the terms of the exchange?

Maybe there was still a ray of hope.

As Morgan was sending Hunt on his way, Ben Clark came riding into the yard.

"What's this peckerwood doin' here?" Clark asked in an angry voice.

"I'll fill you in," Morgan responded. "Tommy brought news about Millie; but now he's got to get back to Bartonville."

"Bartonville?" Clark yelled. "Millie's in Bartonville? What are we waitin' for? Let's go get her!"

"It's not that simple, Ben. She's up that direction somewhere, but Hunt doesn't know the place. So just taking off isn't a good idea."

Clark vaulted from his horse and rushed Hunt, knocking him to the ground. Clark smashed his fist into Hunt's face three times. Blood gushed from Hunt's nose.

"Stop it!" Ruddell yelled from the open front door. "Tommy's got to get back to Bartonville, and he's got to get there in one piece."

Morgan shoved Clark away and onto the ground.

"I'll stop," Clark replied. "But I promise you this, Hunt, if Millie don't get back here as good as when she left, I'll make such a mess outta you that when you get to hell even the devil won't recognize you."

Before Hunt left, Morgan told him to have Robertson at the Red Mountain jailhouse, with Millie, at first light on Tuesday. Morgan would make sure Amos Porter was there to witness the transaction.

"You know he'll have a bunch a' bad guys with him," Hunt called over his shoulder as he rode away. "But I ain't gonna be one of 'em."

Jakes tied the fat outlaw's hands behind his back and the two rode to where the Clydesdales were waiting. Once there, he helped the man dismount and ordered him to sit on the ground.

"Now then, lardgut," Jakes said. "I've got some questions, and the good Lord help you if you don't give me some straight answers."

"Ask all you want, but I don't know nothin' 'bout nothin'."

"You know there's a helpless girl back at the cabin I saw you leavin'. You know she's there with a bunch of pond scum. You know she was brought there by two drunks who work for Al Robertson."

"Seems like you know everthin' already. Don't need me to tell you what you already know."

"I want to know why she was kidnapped, who gave the order, and what they plan to do with her. Even a moron like you should have those answers."

"Don't got no idee why they nabbed 'er. Me an' the other boys was just told to be at the cabin an' keep a eye on 'er 'til Robertson showed up. So far, he ain't showed."

"Where were you headed when you left the cabin?"

"Bartonville. We was 'most outta whiskey, so's I was gonna fetch a few bottles."

"For a skunk, you're a bad liar. Start doin' better with the truth, or you'll know what a skunk feels like when it's skinned alive. How many men does Robertson have workin' for him?"

"He ain't got none. We don't work fer Robertson."

"Then who's your boss?"

"We git our orders from the Bartonville sheriff. We's all deputies, when he needs us to be. You best be careful what you do to me, 'cause you're messin' with the law."

"Just wearin' a star doesn't make you a lawman," Jakes snarled. "Sounds like your sheriff's an outlaw hidin' behind a badge. Whose payroll is he on?"

"I ain't sayin' another word," the round man said emphatically. "I done said too much as is. I ain't sayin' no more. We was all told 'bout you, an' that talkin' to you'd get us kilt. Iffen I say more, 'specially to you, Morgan, I'm dead fer sure."

Jakes was taken aback for a moment. This poor confused soul thought all along that he was Morgan. Maybe Jakes could use this to his advantage.

"Who told you not to talk to me? And how do you know who I am?"

"Ever'one in Bartonville knows 'bout you. You be the hombre what shot down Chad Barton in cold blood 'while back. I was in the posse what chased you when you run scared outta Bartonville. We all thunk you headed fer Mexico 'til that Hunt kid come up here an' figured it was you down at Red Mountain workin' fer that sheep man. I done signed my death warrant by talkin'. But you're gonna be dead, too, an' that's fer true."

"Who's gunnin' for me? And what's the plan to get me?"

"I done told you, I ain't gonna say no more. I'm a dead man fer talkin' to you; you're a dead man fer killin' the Barton boy. So's don't matter none to me iffen you kill me now or I git it later."

"Okay, then," Jakes said, glaring at the man, "I'll go ahead and kill you now. That'll save me the bother of havin' to get you down to Red Mountain. You're death'll be slow, but messy."

Jakes removed a lasso from the rawhide tie on his saddle, put the loop end around one of the man's ankles and cinched it tight. He did the same to the other ankle, using the crook's lasso. Then he tied the loose end of each rope around the necks of the Clydesdales and moved the two horses within ten feet of each other, facing opposite directions.

"I'm glad you decided not to talk anymore," Jakes said with a sinister smile. "I always wondered how fast a man's legs could be torn off his body. Looks like I'm about to find out."

Lying on his back, spread-eagled, the fat man began to shake uncontrollably.

"Awright! Awright! I'll tell you ever'thin' I know. Just don't spook them horses!"

Jakes quickly removed the lassos from the trembling man's legs and pulled him into a sitting position. In a series of nervous jabbers and deep breaths, the story of nabbing Millie to use as barter for Ruddell's ranch came cascading from his beefy lips. Robertson told the gang that Millie was not to be harmed. She was his bargaining chip, and he didn't want her abused in any way. Any man laying a hand on her would be horse-whipped, or worse. Robertson and a bunch of no-goods would bring Millie to Red Mountain for the trade. Hunt would go to Red Mountain to set it all up and get back to Robertson with the day and time.

"I know you're tellin' the truth," Jakes said. "You're too dumb to be makin' this up. Now, get on your horse. We got some ridin' to do."

"Where we goin'? Where you takin' me? I done like you said, an' told you what you wanted to know. I'm gonna be a dead man fer tellin' you them plans. I gotta head fer Mexico 'fore Robertson an' them find out I talked."

"I'm takin' you to Red Mountain and lockin' you up. If you're lucky, when all this is over you'll get a fair trial."

"Oh man, oh man, oh man! Iffen they see me in the Red Mountain jail, they's gonna know fer sure I squealed."

"That's what hogs do," Jakes said, chuckling at his little joke. "But I'll try to keep you hidden away until the dust clears."

"It ain't the dust that'll need to clear—it's the smoke."

"What's that mean? Seems there's more you need to be tellin' me."

"Yeah, they's a heap more, but you gotta promise you'll pertect me iffen I tell you the rest."

"The only promise I'll make is that if you *don't* tell me, you'll need to explain to those Clydesdales the reason they're draggin' your porky legs around."

Sweat dripping from the outlaw's face covered the front of his shirt. He started shaking again.

"Then I got no choice. I gotta take a chance when you hear what I say, you won't let ol' man Barton kill me."

"Barton? What's Barton got to do with this?"

"He's got ever'thin' to do with ever'thin'. He's the one behind it all. It was him who was tryin' to git the sheep man's land. He's the one who was to buy the land iffen Robertson could git the man to sell. It was gonna be fer his boy, Chad, that young'un you kilt up there in Bartonville.

Chad was gonna come down an' run Red Mountain the way his pa runs Bartonville. After the boy died, Barton lost interest in the land fer hisself, but told Robertson he'd back his play iffen he wanted to try runnin' a town. Barton's wife be the sister a' Robertson's wife. They's both dead now."

"That's not tellin' me about smoke. What's your talk about smoke?"

"The ante's gone way up in this here tradin' game. It ain't just the sheep land Barton wants now. Knowin' you be in Red Mountain, he wants you too."

"And how does he think that'll happen?"

"It's all gonna come down at the same time. They's gonna make the trade fer the girl. Robertson's runnin' that show, with 'bout twenty guns 'long side. When that's a done deal, Jason Barton's gonna ride in, with another passel a' men. The Bartonville sheriff's gonna 'rest you, an' haul you back fer a public hangin'."

"Excuse me for soundin' like an echo," Jakes said impatiently. "I still haven't heard about the smoke."

"The smoke's gonna happen iffen, fer any reason, you don't go peaceful-like back to Bartonville. They's all gonna have a torch ready to light up. Iffen you go without a ruckus, that's well an' good. Otherwise, they's gonna burn Red Mountain an' everthin' 'round it. They ain't gonna be a buildin' standin' when it's over."

Jakes had nothing more to say; no more questions to ask. Barton was the real ringleader with Robertson doing the dirty work. Morgan was only half right.

The momentary elation he felt in finding Millie faded quickly. Hearing no harm would befall Millie was reassuring, but considerably outweighed by the prospect of Morgan's needing to either sacrifice his life to a mob bent on hanging him, or watch while an entire community is destroyed.

Knowing Morgan as he did, Jake knew Morgan would surrender himself in order to save Red Mountain. Morgan would reason he had a responsibility to the good people of Red Mountain to keep their lives, their dreams, and their possessions from being decimated. Families had been started and raised in that community; farms and businesses had been built, with dogged determination, by folks who wanted to do nothing more than live in peace and happiness; children had learned to read and write in a schoolhouse, built with a promise the town would always be there; people prayed, and married, and were sent to their eternal rest in a church dedicated to all that's good in the world.

While it grieved him deeply, and angered him to the point of wanting to shout obscenities at the top of his voice, Jakes was certain that to save Red Mountain, Morgan would climb the gallows steps.

One positive aspect existed, however. Due to the providential capturing of a gang member whose only concern was for himself, the plot was uncovered. There may be time to design a counterattack.

Chapter Fifteen

It was early afternoon when Jamison Jakes with his prisoner in tow got back to Red Mountain. From his previous visit to town he knew the location of the jailhouse and headed there, hoping the entry door would be unlocked and a cell key easily found. He was in luck on both counts.

Tying the Clydesdales to a hitching post in front of the livery, Jakes could hear the rhythmic pounding of a hammer hitting an anvil and figured the blacksmith must be working inside. Clemet Morgan had told Jakes that the mayor of Red Mountain, Amos Porter, was also the town blacksmith. Nonetheless, Jakes moved to the door cautiously, announced his presence in a loud voice, and waited for the door to open. When it did, Porter stood in the doorway, shotgun in hand.

"Who are you, fellow, and what do you want?"

"Name's Jamison Jakes. I'm Clemet Morgan's partner from Pueblo, down here to lend a hand. Are you Amos?"

"I truly am," Porter replied, lowering the shotgun. "Sorry about the cannon, but there's a heap of bad things going on around here, and everyone's pretty jumpy."

"There's a whole heap more you don't know, Amos. Let's go inside and I'll fill you in."

Morgan made sure Tommy Hunt had a good start on his trip back to Bartonville before allowing Ben Clark to leave the Rocking Ewe. Morgan didn't want Clark to do anything foolish, like trying to follow Hunt in hopes he'd lead Clark to Millie. Too much was at stake for those kind of games.

Morgan wanted to revisit the Alawanda and search Robertson's house on his way back to Red Mountain, something he hadn't taken time to do when he came across Hunt. He waited fifteen minutes after Clark left before heading out. Seth Ruddell gave Morgan his word he'd stay put at the house, knowing he had to conserve his strength for the trip into Red Mountain to sign over the Rocking Ewe in favor of Robertson. He would ride in a wagon, a mattress on the floorboards with the sides padded all around with blankets.

Searching Robertson's house would probably be a waste of time, but Morgan's experience as a private detective had taught him to be thorough in every investigation, knowing that even the smallest clue might be helpful.

The inside of the house was a mess. In the kitchen,

flies swarmed on uncovered food. Dirty dishes were submerged in a washbasin filled with gray, smelly water. Empty beer bottles cluttered the floor and sideboard. Entering one of the house's two bedrooms, Morgan found the dresser drawers emptied out on the double bed as though the room had been ransacked.

Moving toward the bed to search through the pile, Morgan heard the crunch of glass under his boot. Looking down, realizing he had stepped on a glass picture frame, he picked up the picture. It was a woman in a wedding dress, a very attractive woman, with warm, radiant, smiling eyes. There was writing on the back.

For my darling Al,

Thank you for making me your wife. I will love you forever.

Wanda

Morgan stood transfixed, looking at the picture for a long while. This was Wanda before the lingering sickness came that eventually took her life. She seemed to have been happy on the day the picture was taken, looking forward to a life with Al—having his children and growing old with him.

When did Robertson go sour? Did Wanda know before she died that her husband was conspiring with Jason Barton? Morgan thought not, or at least hoped not. He cleared the clutter from the top of the dresser, removed the jagged pieces of broken glass and placed Wanda's picture in the center.

After going through every room in the house, Morgan found nothing helpful. He took one more look at Wanda's picture, left the house, and continued on his way.

Clark pushed his horse at a gallop and reached Red Mountain quickly. Knowing the morale of the men was fragile at best, he determined to waste no time getting supplies back to the Rocking Ewe range. He had to find a wagon and team of horses. He knew Nell Gainer had recorded all the goods on the stolen wagon, so replacing the items wouldn't require any thought on his part.

Riding up to the livery barn, Clark was surprised and excited to see the two Clydesdales standing quietly in front. He looked around for the wagon. It wasn't there. He dismounted and walked quickly to the horses, rubbing their necks and speaking to them in whispers. Entering the barn, he walked into the middle of a discussion between Porter and Jakes.

"Mr. Porter! Mr. Jakes!" Clark shouted when he saw them. "Where did the horses come from? Where's the wagon?"

"Slow down, son," Porter said. "Jakes here got the horses back, but the wagon's still out there with the bad guys. Jakes saw Millie. She's okay. And she'll stay okay so long as we do what we're supposed to do."

"An' what exactly is that?" Clark asked, his voice cracking with emotion. "If Jakes knows where Millie is, let's go get her! Lord only knows what those crazies might do to her. So let's go!"

Jakes stepped close to Clark, faced him directly, and in a low voice said, "There's some rules we've got to follow to get Millie back. You go on and do what you came to town to do, and we'll take care of the rest."

"Never took either a' you to be cowards. Just tell me where they got her, an' I'll go after her myself."

"Sometimes it takes more courage to do nothin' than to go roarin' into a fight," was Jakes' firm reply. "We've all got our jobs to do; just make sure you do yours. If we keep our wits about us and work together, good can happen."

Clark pondered Jakes' careful, but decisive, response and realized his demands might not result in the outcome he wanted, so he determined to go along with Jakes' plan—at least for then.

While Jakes went back to the jailhouse to check on his prisoner and fetch the crook some food from the Good Grub Café, Porter and Clark quickly hitched the Clydesdales to Porter's wagon and drove it to the general store to load up. Enough daylight remained for Clark to get back to the Rocking Ewe ranch house before dark and deliver the supplies the next morning. He hadn't been told of the threat on Morgan's life or that Morgan was in real jeopardy.

Entering Red Mountain as Clark was leaving, Morgan stopped him for a few minutes to find out what was happening in town. Clark was livid with anger.

"Jakes found Millie. She's okay. He won't tell me where she is. I gotta go get her outta that mess before somethin' bad happens to her."

"That's why he won't tell you. Hightailing after her alone will get you both killed. Just calm down. What else is going on?"

"Jakes caught one of the outlaws and locked him in the hoosegow. He's at Porter's house waitin' for you to show."

"Thanks, Ben. Now get on your way."

Being curious about the man in custody, Morgan decided to stop by the jail on his way to Porter's. Before entering the jailhouse, Morgan pinned on his sheriff's badge.

He found the big man sleeping on a cot in the cell, his hat covering his face. A tray of dirty dishes was on a table next to the cot. The man's snoring was loud and labored. Morgan grabbed a broom handle and ran it quickly over the bars of the cell, creating a clatter that could be heard for a block. The startled man rolled off the cot and onto the floor, yelling a stream of profanities that could also be heard for a block.

"Hey! What's goin' on?" the bad guy asked. "A man can't get no sleep in this place. That Morgan guy comes an' wakes me up so's I can eat, now you come bustin' in here makin' a racket. What kind a' town is this?"

"It's a peaceful town so long as vermin like you stay out of it. Who's Morgan?"

"The yahoo what brung me here. He ain't got no right to do that. He ain't even the law."

Morgan headed toward Porter's house, amused by the thought of how the crook in the lockup assumed Jamison

Jakes was Morgan, and Jakes apparently had made no attempt to set the man straight.

Riding up to the house, Morgan waved broadly to Jakes and Porter sitting on the front porch drinking coffee. Porter stood to shake Morgan's hand while calling through the front door, "Lorna, bring out another cup. Clemet's here."

Within seconds the girl was on the porch, running quickly to Morgan and hugging him tightly, as if she never wanted to let him go. Then she put her cheek against his chest and began to cry.

"Hey," Morgan said gently, "what's the matter, Lorna?"

Without responding she turned quickly and returned to the house, leaving a bewildered Morgan standing alone. Looking at the two men, his face was asking a dozen questions.

"Have a seat, Clem," Jakes said, "we've got a bunch of talkin' to do."

Over the next half hour, Morgan listened intently as Jakes related all that had gone on: searching for Millie, capturing the outlaw, and making him tell what he knew. Morgan, in turn, shared his encounter with Tommy Hunt and Seth Ruddell's decision to pay the ransom.

Jakes saved the worst for last.

"Clem, there's a problem stewin' that's even bigger than gettin' Millie back. Jason Barton has figured out you're the one who plugged his boy and he's comin' down here to take you back to Bartonville to hang. I got that from the load of lard sittin' in the jail. Barton and his gang will be with Robertson when he brings Millie to make the trade. If you don't go along with him peaceful like, he'll burn Red Mountain and everythin' around it to the ground."

"That's what's ailing Lorna," Porter added. "She overheard Jamison and me talking about it and she's been beside herself ever since. Doesn't seem right to me that Barton could just come in here and get whatever he wants. I don't think the people of this town will put up with those kinds of shenanigans."

"There's an old saying that 'might makes right,' " Morgan replied. "If Barton marches in here with a gang of paid killers bent on raising hell, there won't be much the townspeople can, or will, do to stop it."

"You may well be right," Porter said. "That's how he runs the town he named for himself. Some folks just find it easier to look the other way and hide from trouble. But we can't look the other way and hide when your life's at stake. I don't think we're like those spineless Bartonville people. No, sir, not for a minute."

"There's a time to be brave and a time to be smart," Morgan said. "This is a time to be smart. Most people around here don't know me from a monkey. Given the choice of me being hauled off to Bartonville or seeing their homes and businesses burned, they're not going to vote for the monkey."

"Then you've got to hightail it out of here," Porter said. "If they can't find you, they can't kill you."

"You're forgettin' a big hunk of the pie, Amos." Jakes said. "It's a for-sure fact old man Barton's goin' home with a piece of somebody's hide. Won't make a bit of never mind to him whose it is. Sure, he'd love to see Clem swingin' from a rope on the main street of Bartonville, as a reminder of what happens to anyone who crosses him. If Clem isn't here when Barton comes to get him, you can bet your last peso Barton will torch the town, and everythin' for miles around."

"So, we just hand him over to be sacrificed?" Lorna asked, coming to the porch. "Clem's in this because he was asked by one of our good neighbors to come and lend a hand in solving a problem he's facing. He didn't ride in here to make trouble. There has to be something we can do, or at least try to do. We have two days to be ready for those bullies before they get to town. You three can do what you like, but I'm going to try to find some help."

"You're right, Lorna," Porter said, hugging his daughter. "I'll get the word to as many people as I can, and go to the church service tonight. Your brothers can help spread the word too."

"I'll go with Clem to the Rocking Ewe," Lorna said. "He'll need help getting Seth ready for his trip into town."

"And I'll go back to where Millie's bein' held, to keep an eye on her," Jakes said. "Don't worry about that tub of guts at the jail. He has plenty of water, and he can go for a year without eatin' again."

"Sounds good," Morgan said. "Let's all meet back here a little before sunup on Tuesday."

Morgan and Lorna rode along in silence as their horses galloped toward the Rocking Ewe. Lorna stayed a few yards in front. Morgan was impressed with the way she could ride. She had the remarkable talent of appearing to be a genteel lady one minute and a tough frontierswoman the next. She could be warm softness, or chilly hardness, depending on the situation.

Morgan was glad he had come to Red Mountain, was pleased to have met so many good, honest, and caring people. He could spend the rest of his days here, he was thinking. Here among these good people, in this good place. Here, with this woman of leather and lace.

Then he became amused in a morbid way, remembering his days—wherever he was—might well be numbered.

Suddenly, and seemingly for no reason, Lorna reined to a quick stop. She dismounted, walked her horse to a fallen tree and sat on the massive trunk, pensive and reflective. Morgan followed suit and sat silently, looking at the ground in front of him. He knew Lorna would speak when she was ready.

"I knew a man would come into my life someday, and I would know him the moment I saw him," Lorna said quietly. "For what it's worth, that moment came when I laid eyes on you the first day. I knew you were that man. I don't expect you to say anything. Not a word. But I want you to know: I love you, Clemet Morgan. I've loved you for a long time, even before we met.

"You know by now I'm a woman who speaks her mind and I know many men don't find that attractive in a woman."

"Lorna, I find everything about you attractive," Morgan said, still looking at the ground. "You're a beautiful woman, but beyond that, I admire your strength and courage. Just now I was enjoying watching you ride. I like the sound of your voice so much I hear it in my dreams. When I saw you with the children at the Harvest Festival, I let my mind run wild, imagining you were my wife and those were our children."

Only then did they allow their eyes to meet. Standing slowly, they faced one other and Morgan took Lorna in his arms. In a moment of sweet bliss they embraced, putting aside the looming crisis which seemed destined to destroy their community and their newfound love.

When Jakes reached the cabin where Millie was being held captive, he found the place eerily quiet. There were no horses and, although it was almost dark, no lamps were lit in the cabin, nor was smoke coming from the chimney. Jakes moved to a position that allowed him to be certain no one was about, then crept to the window for a look inside.

Nothing. Going to the side door of the cabin, Jakes tried the knob. Finding the door unlocked, he drew his Colt and cautiously entered. The room was in total disarray. Jakes touched the cook stove with the palm of his hand and felt slight warmth. From this he figured the stove had been used some hours before, but hadn't been stoked. Large boxes of food and other materials were stacked against the walls. The stolen contents of the supply wagon had been left behind.

Why had the thieves left in such a hurry? Were they spooked when the fat man didn't return with the whiskey? Had plans changed, so the proposed siege of Red Mountain would be happening sooner than expected? Maybe Tommy Hunt had second thoughts about his feelings of guilt and told Al Robertson what really went on between Morgan and Hunt. One thing was certain: Jakes needed to get back to Red Mountain pronto, at first light.

When they arrived at the Rocking Ewe, Lorna and Morgan found Ruddell resting comfortably on the sofa. Ruddell said Ben Clark had taken the supplies to the herdsmen earlier in the day and should be returning within the hour. Lorna went into the kitchen, started a fire in the cook stove and searched for something to make a hot meal. By the time Clark arrived, Lorna had put together a supper of jerky gravy and biscuits, boiled turnips, and coffee. The four savored each bite of this simple fare as if it might be their last meal together.

After supper, Morgan asked Clark what was happening on the range.

"It's not goin' good," Clark responded. "The two men who said they'd stay for a few days had second thoughts an' headed home. Only got seven left. Harry knows Swift Eagle an' the Navajos will hang in, but a couple of other married men are gettin' squeamish."

"I want to be fair to those men," Ruddell said. "No need for anyone to stay out there if I'm turning everything over to Robertson. Those sheep will be his; let him worry about what happens to them. Clemet, you go out there in the morning and tell everyone to go on home. Take what money I've got here in the house and split it up among them as a final payday."

"That sounds more than fair to me," Morgan said. "And I'll warn them about Jason Barton's plans as well. They'll need to be on guard."

Chapter Sixteen

Jason Barton wasn't born bad. However, a number of bad things happened in his life that molded him into the mean, sour and vindictive man he had become. Barton's parents left their ancestral home in England for America because of the potato famine that ravaged the British Isles for a decade beginning in 1845.

They arrived in New York City in the winter of 1852. Sixteen-year-old Jason—having lived a life of privilege—didn't fit well into the rough and ragged Irish ghetto environment where the family was forced to settle. The Irish were, to Jason's thinking, nothing more than potato-grubbers whose tedious labor had made it possible for the Barton family to have lived the good life, moving at will between their country estate and their London townhouse.

In order to survive in his new environment, his private

school education was quickly replaced by learning the ways of the street. He watched in despair as his father turned to heavy drinking, leading to bouts of depression. Depression won the final battle when Barton's father climbed to the aqueduct atop High Bridge and plunged a hundred and forty feet into the Harlem River. Later, when his mother married a German shoe cobbler who didn't want a teenage boy in his life, Jason was left to fend for himself. He left the city and headed west.

Having no skills as a craftsman, for eight years Barton moved from place to place and job to job until the outbreak of the Civil War. Being in Chicago in 1862, he signed on with the Seventy-second Illinois Infantry Regiment Volunteers, a group known as the Hancock Guards. Barton was twenty-five years old, angry at the world and everyone in it.

He didn't care for Army life and would have deserted early on if it hadn't been for the killing part. His rifle and his bayonet became his best friends. He gave them names and talked to them as if they were human. He christened the rifle 'Big Shot,' the bayonet 'Cut Up,' and created games of competition for them. He had no real-life comrades.

Barton was older than most in his regiment and quickly moved up through the ranks and got his sergeant's stripes. Put in charge of a troop of ragtag misfits, he christened them "Barton's Bloody Boys." They became infamous overnight for their ruthless—and sometimes senseless—combat tactics.

At the end of the war, Barton was again faced with the prospect of drifting to scratch out an existence; but he wanted no more of that. Realizing he had come of age as a man, and had developed a knack for being a leader of men, he decided to take advantage of both. The infantry troop he commanded began with thirty-two men. At the war's end, death or desertion had reduced that number by half. Those remaining were the worst of the bad. Most were illiterate, but all could make their marks. Their courage came from a bottle, their pleasure from inflicting pain.

Barton's plan was simple. He would map a zigzag route west, lead his band of bullies from place to place, helping themselves to anything and everything they wanted. Law enforcement on the frontier fell mostly to the Army, and all units were short of men. Crime in any form was very profitable.

Barton had long admired William Quantrill and his raiders. Although Quantrill joined the Civil War on the side of the Confederacy, he soon grew impatient with the strict regimentation of Army life and formed a band of guerilla fighters. In addition to fighting Union troops, the Quantrill gang robbed mail coaches, trains and banks, and rustled cattle. They also murdered people suspected of being loyal to Abraham Lincoln, and slaughtered captured Union soldiers. By the time Quantrill died of a shot wound in June 1865, his raiders had been reduced to a paltry thirty-three members.

Barton considered himself smarter than Quantrill and reasoned, with a much smaller gang, he could strike banks and mail coaches quicker and with greater frequency. Another lesson learned from Quantrill was not to be confined in one region. Whereas Quantrill's mayhem was restricted to communities in Missouri and Kansas, Barton chose a more random approach—but always moved westward.

The Barton gang was under total control of their leader and each member knew his life would be snuffed in an instant if he ever crossed the boss. Barton, in his own fashion, was a clever outlaw. He would plan all the heists, but never participated in carrying them out. He was never seen with his men. They all knew if they were captured, they were on their own.

Rather than sharing a cut of the loot from the robberies, Barton paid his gang a salary on the first day of every month. Each was given a little extra if the haul was larger than expected. When the gang returned from a caper with saddlebags filled with swag, Barton transferred it to one of two large metal boxes strapped to a mule. He kept the boxes locked to make the money doubly safe from his men. He had them believing that if anyone but Barton touched the boxes, let alone tried to open them, a massive explosion would occur, blowing the intruder to bits along with the money. The men kept their distance from the boxes.

After almost three years of accumulating a fortune in stolen gold, silver and greenbacks, Jason Barton and crew found themselves in the northwest corner of New Mexico Territory.

After many days of riding through the arid, desert-like countryside they had seen only one person: a man headed for Santa Fe to file a claim on free land the territorial government was making available. Anyone proving they had sufficient resources to productively develop the land could get a grant. Barton invited the man to join him for a meal. After getting all the information needed to file a claim, Barton shot the man, stole his money, and ordered his cronies to dispose of the body before setting up camp.

In the midst of the most beautiful country he had ever seen, Barton felt it was time to stop running and settle down—settle down in a town he would build, surrounded by miles of rangeland he would own.

Santa Fe had two banks. Barton deposited half of his fortune into each and submitted the bank receipts as part of his land-grant application. The territorial decision-makers were so impressed by Barton's show of wealth and his plans to create a town in the center of newly established cattle and farm land, they awarded him sixty-four thousand acres. One hundred square miles to do with as he saw fit.

Before leaving Santa Fe, Barton contracted with an architect and a surveyor to begin work designing the new buildings, and plotting parcels which would be allotted to the ranchers and farmers who would be drawn to the area by the new town. The first structure would be Barton's house—a mansion from which he would oversee his domain. He also commissioned designs for a saloon, a general store, a boarding house, a post office, a livery stable, a school, and a church. While he didn't give any truck to religion, he thought a church would be a nice touch.

The architect would find a contractor who, in turn, would hire the laborers to do the work. Bonuses were promised if the town could be built and be usable within six months.

All of this generated quite a stir throughout Santa Fe and soon Barton was known on sight by everyone. He wallowed in the attention he received, especially in the evenings when the dance hall girls and good old boys buttered up Barton nonstop in exchange for drinks. For the first time since he was a child—before the bleak years—he felt important. Small matter it was ill-gotten wealth that catapulted him into the limelight.

Wagonloads of building materials were delivered to the site Barton selected for the new town, which he named "Bartonville."

As Barton hoped, when the town was completed, people from all walks of life began arriving. Almost immediately renters were operating the general store, saloon, boarding house and livery stable. Barton retained ownership of the buildings as well as the range and farmland. Homesteaders who grew crops or raised cattle on Barton land paid him a percentage of the income they received for their labor.

When the preacher and schoolteacher were hired, the

congregation and the parents of the schoolchildren paid a monthly rental for facility use. Jason Barton was indeed a rich man—becoming richer.

A family named Hunt moved into the new settlement to become proprietors of the boarding house. George and Blanche Hunt had three children: Annabelle, Wanda and Tommy. Annabelle, in her early twenties, was the eldest. Wanda was seventeen, Tommy a two-year-old toddler.

Annabelle was pretty, vivacious and tolerant to a fault. She immediately caught the eye of Jason Barton. Although he was twenty years her senior, she was flattered by the attention he gave her and soon agreed to be his wife. Their marriage was the first ceremony performed in the Bartonville Community Church. The reception that followed at Barton's mansion was lavish.

Wanda worked as a cleaner and cook in her parents' boarding house and was well thought of by the folks staying there. Of the six sleeping rooms, full-time residents occupied four. Two rooms were available for day-to-day renters.

One of the regular overnight guests—staying once a week—was a man named Al Robertson. Robertson ran a weekly freight delivery route from Santa Fe to Farmington and the creation of a layover place provided a welcomed break. His stops in Bartonville became longer and longer as more and more hours were spent in conversation with Wanda at the end of the day. After six months of courting on an irregular schedule, Robertson quit his hauling job, moved into the boarding house, and asked Wanda to marry him. Although her parents thought Wanda was too young for marriage, and she could do better than the likes of Robertson, they reluctantly agreed.

Soon after the wedding, Al and Wanda Robertson moved from Bartonville to Red Mountain and bought a small ranch, using money Al had saved over the years. Barton offered Robertson a good paying job as rent collector, but Robertson was determined to prove he could make it on his own.

Less than a year after their marriage the Bartons had a child, a son they named Chad. The boy was showered with the best of everything Barton's riches could buy. Annabelle, concerned they were raising a spoiled brat, pleaded with her husband to dote less on the boy.

In the fifteenth year of their marriage, Annabelle contracted an incurable disease and died soon after. Barton, in a perpetual state of anger and depression after Annabelle's premature death, became impossible to be around. Chad Barton became his father's solace and nothing the boy wanted was ever denied.

However, on the day he lay dead in the dust of Bartonville's main street, Chad Barton wanted something his father couldn't give him: Millie Ruddell.

Chapter Seventeen

A lot of ground had to be covered before Tuesday morning. Amos Porter and his sons were frustrated and angered by the response they received from the townspeople and other families in the community. Rather than rallying around the mayor in his call for solidarity to meet the threat that could possibly lead to the destruction of Red Mountain, the alarm went unheeded. Some chose to believe the threat was not real; others said they would pack their belongings and head to a safe place. No one expressed any willingness to stand up against the Bartonville bullies.

Porter had one bit of success by insisting the Sunday church time be given over to an open discussion of the crisis that was escalating within the otherwise peaceful community. For those new to the area, Porter traced the history of Red Mountain and for the old-timers he reviewed memorable highlights. John Bundy, believing in the collective strength of his neighbors, committed to help the cause if someone would tell him what to do. On the other hand, pig farmer Jim Leklem argued angrily that this was Seth Ruddell's problem. Ruddell brought this grief to Red Mountain and now it was his job to take care of it.

Reverend Grassley interrupted the heated discussion with prayer and spontaneously led the congregation in singing all six verses of the old hymn, "Be Thou Ever Near." Grassley asked protection for Millie Ruddell and her safe return. He prayed fervently that the Lord would lead Clemet Morgan to turn himself over to the Barton gang to save the town and that Morgan would seek salvation so he could enter heaven immediately after the hanging.

They reached a tentative conclusion. Ruddell should give his land to Robertson in exchange for Millie; and to save Red Mountain from being destroyed by the Bartonville gang, Morgan should give his life.

Disturbed by the dire events, yet bolstered by their newfound love, Morgan and Lorna sat for hours in the porch swing of the Rocking Ewe ranch house sharing stories of their lives. Morgan already knew a great deal about Lorna from talking with her and her parents; not so, the other direction.

Lorna found it strangely odd that she had fallen in love with a man about whom she knew so little. As the night wore on, however, she heard nothing from Morgan to make her believe she had made a mistake in revealing her feelings. To the contrary, each story showed the strength of his character and the depth of his passion for fairness, justice and truth.

In these moments of sharing, Morgan dealt with emotions foreign to him. He had no frame of reference for the thoughts racing through his head. He had never uttered the phrase "I love you" to anyone. When he heard those words come from his lips, he was in a surreal space, unmarked by time. So he repeated the words again—then again, chuckling—as he realized the amazing pleasure of expressing his love. Looking deeply into Lorna's eyes, he said "I love you" one more time.

Finally, encouraged by the gentle swaying of the swing and the fatigue racking their bodies, they fell asleep, Lorna's head on Morgan's shoulder. When a rooster's crow announced morning's arrival, they held each other for a moment and prepared to face an uncertain day.

Jamison Jakes pushed his horse hard as he dared in his dash to Red Mountain to tell Morgan that Millie had been moved to some unknown location and she was no longer at the cabin where he had seen her.

Being unfamiliar with the territory, and wanting to get to Red Mountain quickly, Jakes stayed on the main road. However, a number of miles from town, without warning Jakes' horse turned suddenly onto a bridal path branching from the main trail and slowed to a walk. No amount of coaxing or cajoling on Jakes' part influenced the horse to change direction.

Two hundred yards into the woods, the horse stopped and stood motionless. In the crisp silence of the morning, Jakes heard the muffled sound of voices in the distance. He quickly dismounted, led his horse deeper into the thick stand of pine trees and tied the reins to a trunk. With one measured step after another, Jakes slipped like a shadow between the drooping limbs, moving steadily toward the voices.

In a clearing on the upward side of a hill not far away, he saw a large group of unshaven, dirty men, working at tying rolled-up rags onto the ends of short sticks and stacking them in piles. Near this activity, a woman was sitting on the ground with her ankles bound together and her hands tied behind her back.

It was Millie! Jakes reasoned her captors were moving her toward Red Mountain a few miles each day, so by Tuesday they would be within a short distance of town and nothing would interfere with getting to the exchange meeting on time.

Returning to his horse, Jakes was reassured in knowing that Millie was safe for the time being, although probably scared out of her wits. Once Jakes mounted, the horse turned without prompting and walked back along the path to the road.

It was early Sunday afternoon before Morgan reached the herd. Lorna had wanted to ride out with him but he convinced her she was needed at the ranch to care for Seth Ruddell. Ruddell had slept hard during the night but was slow to respond to Morgan's attempts to wake him. He would be alert for a few minutes then lapse into a deep sleep and remain there for long periods. Lorna placed wet washcloths on his brow, and kept his dry, cracked lips moist. During the night he experienced a period of delirium, speaking to persons unknown to Morgan or Lorna. Ben Clark expressed a concern that Ruddell might die before Tuesday. His question as to what would happen in that event went unanswered.

It took a half-hour for Harry Samuels to get the crew together in one place so Morgan could to talk to them. The somber look on Morgan's face signaled the news he had to tell wasn't good. They stood in a semicircle in front of Morgan, looking first at him, then at each other, then back at Morgan as they waited for him to speak.

On his ride out, Morgan had given a lot of thought as to what he would and would not say to the men. First, he thanked them for their loyalty to Ruddell, and the honest, hard work they had done for the Rocking Ewe. Then he told them the ranch was being sold to Robertson at dawn on Tuesday, the signing to take place in Red Mountain.

"I've got your pay here with me," Morgan continued, reaching into his saddlebag and pulling out a stack of greenbacks. "It may not be all you have coming, but it's what Seth had at the ranch. I'll give it to Harry and he'll count it out. Each of you will get an equal share."

"What happens to the sheep?" Samuels asked. "Do we just leave 'em here to fend for themselves?"

"That's what we'll have to do. Pull down a big section of the fence, and let's hope they find enough grass and water to stay alive. If Robertson wants the sheep, he can come out here and find them."

"This ain't makin' no sense," Samuels complained. "They's gotta be more goin' on here than you're tellin' us. We got a right to know the whole story. Why would Seth be sellin' his ranch to a man who come out here and killed two a' us in cold blood?" The other men mumbled their agreement with Samuels' question. "I'll say again. This ain't makin' no sense."

Morgan was quiet for a few minutes; he needed time to think this through. Riding out, he'd decided to just matter-of-factly tell the men the ranch was being sold, and they would be out of work. Standing in front of them now, seeing the looks on their faces reflecting both hurt and confusion, he knew Samuels was right: They did deserve the whole truth.

He reminded the men why he was in town, of Robertson's quest of getting ownership of the Rocking Ewe and Robertson's attempt to put Ruddell out of business. Morgan placed the saga of Jed Nooley's death and Lester Hobson being wrongfully accused into perspective. To advance his sinister goal, Robertson had murdered Sheriff Gainer and two Rocking Ewe crew members. When all else failed, Robertson had his goons kidnap Millie and was using her as ransom to get Ruddell's land.

"That stinkin' polecat!" Samuels shouted. "He can't git away with that. We won't let him git away with that, will we fellers? Morgan, you be the actin' sheriff. Swear us in an' we'll hunt down that skunk an' string him up!"

The other men shouted their agreement.

"Hold on, Harry. You're right, as acting sheriff, it's my job to work all this out, and I really appreciate your offer. But you've got to know what we're up against. If it was just Robertson, that wouldn't be a problem; but he's coming into town with a whole bunch of other skunks to back him up. These lamebrains would sooner kill you than give you the time of day. Seth doesn't want anything done that will get Millie hurt. Robertson's gone loco. Anyone who gets in his way could be killed. So you men stay out of it. Seth is stoved up so bad he'll need to go into town in a wagon. And he'll have to stay in the wagon to do the deed signing. Any funny business and he'll be dead meat."

"So, you're tellin' us to go on home, an' do nothin'."

"Yes, you need to go home—especially if you have families. Get them to a safe place before Tuesday. If you live alone, go somewhere you know you'll be okay."

Morgan felt compelled to share the other half of the story. These men needed to be prepared to protect themselves, and their families, from Jason Barton and his bloodthirsty pack. The gang would be hell-bent on following whatever orders Barton gave in his determination to avenge his son's death.

As deliberately and completely as he had discussed Millie's abduction, Morgan spelled out his killing of Chad Barton—and why and how it happened. He told them Jason Barton planned to take him to Bartonville to be hanged.

"I've learned that if I refuse to go, or run away, the entire Red Mountain region will be reduced to ashes. Barton will have dozens of men with him to make sure the job gets done. But he could nab me and still torch the town and everything around it. That's why you have to go away—and stay away—until all this is over."

To a man, the herders were in a state of stunned disbelief. Swift Eagle was the only one moving as he interpreted the saga to his three comrades in sign language and Navajo.

"So, that's it," Morgan concluded. "If a couple of you pull a hole in the fence as you ride out, I'd be much obliged. Take your dogs. You're all good men. It's been my pleasure to know you."

Morgan rode out a half-mile or so before looking back. The men were busy gathering up belongings and watching Samuels count out their pay. One man—Swift Eagle—sat astride his horse looking toward Morgan. As Morgan caught this last glimpse of the men and sheep he had come to know and appreciate, Swift Eagle waved his arm broadly in a final farewell.

Getting back to the Rocking Ewe ranch house just before dark, Morgan was disappointed to find Lorna gone. Clark explained Ruddell's condition had improved considerably.

One of Lorna's brothers had ridden out and Lorna left soon after to go back to town. She didn't give Clark a reason.

Morgan sat on the edge of the bed and visited a while with Ruddell, telling the old man what had transpired out on the range, and his decision to let the sheep wander. Then the two men made some loose plans for the job of getting ready for the trip to Red Mountain. Since their meeting with Porter and Jakes was scheduled for early Tuesday morning, Morgan suggested that he, Clark and Ruddell make the trip on Monday. This would give Ruddell time to rest before the dawn showdown with Robertson on Tuesday. Clark had gone to bed in the barn while Morgan and Ruddell were talking.

After dousing the lamp in Ruddell's bedroom and closing the door, Morgan sat on the living room sofa in darkness for a long while, lost in thought. He then lit the kitchen lamp and sat at the table.

Taking a pen in hand, he dipped the point in an ink bottle and slid a blank sheet of paper in front of him. After a minute of pensive thought, he printed on the top of the page. Last Will and Testament of Clemet Morgan. He had learned how to prepare a will, and the importance of having one, from a client who was a lawyer.

He figured it was time to get his affairs in order. Then it hit him. In this somber moment of introspection, he realized how little he had in life and how few people he had to leave anything to. His detective agency was successful, but not very profitable. The last time he inquired as to the money he had in his Pueblo bank account, the amount was less than five hundred dollars. For his trip to Red Mountain, he had withdrawn half of that.

After including the obligatory legal jargon of "being of sound mind" and such, Morgan wrote:

All of my earthly goods and possessions, both personal and professional, I leave to my business partner, Jamison Jakes.

There it was. In fewer than two dozen words, Morgan had disposed of a lifetime of work and memories, and any hope for the future. After reading the brief statement a few more times, however, Morgan realized he did have something else. He dipped the pen in the ink and made one more brief bequest:

And to Lorna Porter, I give my heart and soul and all the love I have ever possessed, knowing she will treasure it, until we meet again.

After signing and dating the short document, he waited for the ink to dry then carefully folded the paper and placed it on the table in front of him. He would ask Porter to sign as a witness and make sure the will got to Pueblo for filing.

Chapter Eighteen

Because of Seth Ruddell's restless night, Clemet Morgan decided to wait as long as possible before starting the Red Mountain trip. Ben Clark had done a good job padding the wagon so Ruddell's broken body wouldn't feel the pain inflicted by hitting the bumps and ruts plaguing the well-worn road. Before they began their journey, Clark threw in extra blankets in case Ruddell wanted more warmth.

As the wagon plodded along with Clark driving, Morgan followed a few yards behind, riding his gelding. He loved his horse. He'd bought him as a colt from a breeder in Illinois for a cheap price, having been judged worthless due to his stubborn and ornery disposition. It took a lot of work on Morgan's part to bring him around, but once they agreed that Morgan was the one in charge, they became best friends. Morgan knew Jamison Jakes would care for the horse as though it were his own.

Morgan's mind drifted to the day he first came down this road heading for the Rocking Ewe; his first meeting with Harry Samuels and Swift Eagle; and his surprise in finding Ruddell and Millie were the ones harassed by Chad Barton.

This seemed like years ago. Morgan shook his head in disbelief, realizing all that had happened since he rode into Red Mountain had occurred in only six weeks. Six weeks of frustration mixed with fun; laughter mixed with tears. Friendships bond quickly when the heat of conflict fuses them together. He came to Red Mountain with no one in his life, except Jakes, whom he considered a true friend. In six short weeks he had found friends who could last a lifetime, and a love that could span eternity.

A sudden cloudburst drenched the trio a few miles from town, but the night showed signs of clearing. As the soggy trio reached the outskirts of Red Mountain some stars became visible and a half moon shone from time to time through the clouds, silhouetting the buildings of the town.

Other than some intermittent moonlight, the quiet village was in complete darkness. Not a flicker of light came from any building; not even a barking dog broke the eerie silence.

"This is really spooky," Clark said in a whisper. "Where in thunket are the people?"

Morgan, now in the lead, headed the small caravan

toward Porter's house. To their shared relief, a light was shining behind the closed drapes. Through a gap, Porter could be seen sitting in his favorite chair, smoking a pipe. He was talking with someone. Morgan hoped it was Lorna.

Not wanting to startle those in the house by walking to the door unannounced, Morgan called out, "Hello, the house! Clemet Morgan here!" The front door opened almost immediately and a man stood holding a lamp. It was Jakes.

"Hey, man!" Jakes all but shouted. "Glad you got here early. Who's with you? Get in this house and tell us what's goin' on."

Within a few minutes, Ruddell had been carried in and propped up, half asleep, on the sofa. Porter brought water and made Ruddell drink it, much against his will. Ruddell needed to stay awake long enough to hear Jakes tell he'd seen Millie looking tense and fearful, but otherwise well. There would be no time in the morning to do anything other than go to the jailhouse and wait for Robertson and his squad to ride in, bringing Millie with them.

"Where's all the people?" Clark wanted to know "We didn't see no one when we rode in."

"Everyone who lives in town is gone. I sent them away to stay with friends and neighbors," Porter answered. "And by dawn, I want you gone, too, young man."

"That won't happen, Mayor. I'm gonna be right there with Seth when Millie comes in. I plan to take care of 'em both, soon as all this business is done. She don't know it yet but Millie and me are gonna be hitched real quick."

Ruddell feebly nodded his agreement.

"Is Robertson's henchman still in jail?" Morgan asked.

"Nope," Jakes replied. "I moved him down to the general store, and put him in a food locker. The locker will most likely be empty by mornin', but he kept yellin' how Robertson would kill him if he knew he'd been talkin' with the law."

"Do you know where Lorna is?" Morgan asked Porter. "If she's not too far away, I'd like to talk with her."

"I'm sorry, Clemet," Porter answered in a sad tone. "She took Elsie and the boys and headed west. Most likely to Bundy's, but they're a good ways out. Could be she'd stop closer in, but I've got no way of knowing where."

"That's okay, Amos. Just tell her I said she needs to be strong through all this and, if by some miracle I get out of the pickle I got us all into, I'll be coming back to Red Mountain."

Porter's response was a deep sigh that conveyed more than words could say.

Morgan reached into his shirt pocket and pulled out the will he had written earlier.

"Got a big favor to ask of you, Amos," Morgan said, unfolding the piece of paper. "This is my last will and testament. It needs to be witnessed and filed with the county clerk in Pueblo to make it legal. Would you sign as the witness, and see that it gets filed?"

A dark pall of reality filled the room. No one spoke or breathed. In all the preparation for Millie's return, sight was lost for a moment of the fact that Morgan was going to die. Jason Barton was on his way and if all went in Barton's favor, Morgan would be swinging from the end of a rope in just a couple of days.

"Jamison, I'm leaving everything I have to you and Maryalice," Morgan said, breaking the silence. "You can do what you want with the business. You're a good man and a good detective, so I know you'll make a go of it. There are no outstanding debts, but Clarence Bigelow still owes us quite a bit. It's all in the ledger. There's a little money in the bank that should come in handy, what with your family growing."

"I can't believe this," Clark blurted out. "We're sittin' here talkin' 'bout Clemet dyin', like we was watchin' a horseshoe tossin' match. They's got to be somethin' we can do."

"We're in a tight spot, Ben," Morgan answered. "For all his meanness, Jason Barton is a cunning man. He understands how people's fear can be used to get him what he wants. I experienced firsthand how folks in Bartonville live in constant fear of the man. We've seen how he turned Al Robertson into a kidnapper and killer. If we don't do his bidding, dozens of people here in Red Mountain are going to lose their business, their homes, and maybe even their lives.

"Just for show, Barton will make sure there's a trial before I'm hung. He wants it to look like everything's being done within the law. He's fooled a lot of people for a long time, making them think he's a respectable, upstanding citizen. He needs a phony trial to prove what a fair man he is and that he runs a law-abiding town. It'll be a kangaroo court at best.

"My hope is I'll at least get a chance to say something in my defense before I climb those thirteen steps. Who knows, if I'm clever and convincing enough with my story, even a Barton jury may turn me loose."

Morgan's broad smile told the others he didn't believe that would ever happen.

It was useless for the men to try for sleep, so they didn't. Even Ruddell was awake for most of the night. Porter boiled a pot of strong coffee and made sandwiches, but no one could eat.

Morgan wandered through the house and found Lorna's room. It was a neat, well-decorated space that perfectly reflected her total personality. Paintings on the walls were bright and cheery; the bed comforter had an appliqué of children playing a circle game; needlepoint cloths covered the dresser top and crocheted doilies were on the arms of an overstuffed chair.

On a shelf above the head of the bed was a family of stuffed animals, looking happy and content. A large oval rug was braided with multicolored cotton strips, and the frame of a full-length mirror covering a large portion of the closet door had been painted a vibrant white.

Looking inside the closet, Morgan was amused by the

number, and types, of outfits on display. One side was filled with hanging dresses: some frilly, some formal, but mostly just attractive dresses that might be worn anywhere, for any occasion. On pegs above the dresses were bonnets of all sizes and colors, some with artificial flowers, some with ribbons. The floor below the dresses was covered with a dozen or more pairs of shoes: high-tops with hooks, high-tops with laces, black patent leather, white patent leather, and slippers.

By total contrast, the other half of the closet held leather and denim jackets, leather vests and pants, plaid work shirts, fancy dress shirts, and chaps. The pegs held leather and cloth cowboy hats, a variety of belts with large buckles and a collection of leather quirts. The floor on that side of the closet was home to a number of pairs of highly polished boots and three pairs of beaded moccasins.

"Is it any wonder I love this girl?" Morgan mumbled to himself as he closed the door and headed downstairs.

The large clock, striking the hour of five, roused everyone from their private thoughts and each, in his own way, tried to put on a positive face. Clark had been to the wagon, making sure it was dry before they put Ruddell in the bed. The morning was chilly, so Clark brought the blankets inside and draped them over chairs in front of the fire.

Porter made a third pot of coffee and, despite what lay ahead of them when the sun came up, each had a sandwich. Even Ruddell managed to eat a few bites and sip some hot coffee.

Jakes had been deeper in thought than the others, and finally spoke.

"Amos, I want you to swear me in as Clem's deputy, and give me a star to wear for this meetin' were havin'. In fact, swear all of us in. When we face this gang of crooks, let's do it as lawmen, not as civilians. Some of those snakes may have second thoughts if they know they're dealin' with the law. And if we need to kill any of them, those stars will give us license."

Porter thought the idea was excellent and within a few minutes Sheriff Morgan had four deputies, all wearing shiny badges. Shortly after Harold Gainer volunteered to be Red Mountain's sheriff, Porter ordered six badges. The extras were in case a posse was ever needed. This would be the first. Both Ruddell and Porter took the oath, along with Jakes and Clark. Porter stood in front of a mirror to administer the oath to himself. He made the appointments official by recording the names and date in the town registry.

With the first hint of daylight, Clark and Jakes hitched the horses to the wagon, carried Ruddell out, made him as comfortable as possible, and covered him with blankets warmed by the fire.

Morgan and Jakes led the way on horseback. Clark drove the wagon, sitting alongside Porter. And with Ruddell on his bed of blankets, they began moving slowly toward the jailhouse to wait for Robertson and his gang.

Chapter Nineteen

Arriving at the jailhouse, Ben Clark unhitched the horses, took them to the back of the building, and tied them to trees. If the situation got nasty and shooting happened, a spooked draft horse was the last thing they wanted. Morgan had decided the meeting, and the exchange, should be held in the open rather than inside the small room. This would allow Ruddell to stay in the wagon, propped to a sitting position and covered with blankets, during the deed transfer.

The wagon was placed in the middle of the street facing west, the direction from which Robertson would be coming. Clark and Porter sat on the wagon seat while Morgan and Jakes stayed mounted, taking positions on each side at the front of the wagon.

An orange glow, through the early morning haze, gave promise of a sunny day.

A nearby rooster's crowing made everyone jump a little. There hadn't been a sound for many minutes. All eyes were fixed on the horizon in front of them as they impatiently waited for some movement, some sign telling them Millie was on her way.

After another half-hour of anticipation, a lone horseman came into view at the end of the long street. He pulled the brim of his hat down to protect his eyes from the sun, now brilliant in the eastern sky. As the rider slowly approached, Morgan recognized the man. It was Tommy Hunt.

A furious Clark stood quickly, and shouted, "Where's Millie? She was to be here by now! Where is she?"

"Simmer down, Ben!" Morgan demanded. "Let the boy tell us why he's here."

"Al sent me in to see if you'd made it. He weren't gonna come in unless you was here waitin' for him. He wanted me to see how many a' you they was, an' let you know that he's got twenty men backin' him, an' he don't want no funny stuff goin' on."

"Well, you can see we're here, and you can count how many of us there are," Morgan replied curtly. "Let him know we're all sworn lawmen. We don't want any funny stuff from him either."

It was then Hunt noticed the badges on each man.

"Okay, Sheriff," Hunt said. "You gotta know I ain't a part a' this. I'm just here 'cause Al made me come. I'll report you're here waitin' with Seth, how many a' you they is, an' that you're all wearin' badges. But after that—I'm gone. I hope to never see Al again."

With this, Hunt quickly spurred his horse to leave, then stopped and turned back.

"They's one more thin' you need to know. Out there, just behind Al an' his crew, is my brother-in-law Jason. He's got twice the number a' men Al's got, an' they's twice as mean. They all got torches ready to light, an' Jason's gonna burn Red Mountain down just for spite. He knows Al can't never come back here an' be the town boss."

"Thanks, Tommy," Morgan said quietly. "You best get on back there now and tell Robertson we're waiting."

As the boy rode away, each man put what he had just heard into a personal context.

Morgan realized the plight was no longer an either-or situation between Barton and him. It was now a do-and-die. Barton would wait for Ruddell to sign the deed over to Robertson, making sure ownership of the Rocking Ewe got legally transferred, and then take Morgan to Bartonville to hang while his henchmen torched Red Mountain.

Ruddell wanted only one thing: to get Millie back safely. He felt his life slipping away with each labored breath, and prayed he could live long enough to see her again. He knew Clark would take good care of her.

Porter's very soul was in distress. He had dedicated much of his life to Red Mountain. This is where he lived and worked and raised a loving family; where he had devoted his personal time and effort making it a good, safe community; where he and his wife had hoped to be for the remainder of their lives. He was heartsick as he realized the town would go up in smoke.

Jakes thought of home, his wife Maryalice and their son Daniel, and wondered if he was a father again. In working with Morgan, Jakes totally respected and admired the man. Morgan was his best friend. Now he felt powerless to help.

Another half-hour passed.

Then the parade began.

From a distance, a cluster of riders came into view with Robertson leading the pack a few yards in front. Behind him was Millie, riding between two men. She was blindfolded and her hands tied behind her back. Following were the twenty grungy men Hunt promised would be there.

When this collection of desert vermin got within thirty feet of the wagon, Morgan raised his hand.

"That's close enough," he said firmly. "No one goes any farther, except Robertson and Millie."

The saddle tramps looked at their leader. Robertson gave a signal. They stopped.

"Where's my grandpa?" Millie yelled. "I want to see my grandpa!"

"I'm here, Millie, in the wagon," Ruddell said in a feeble voice.

"Take the blindfold off so she can see him," Morgan

insisted. "Seth has done everything he was told to do; including letting you steal his ranch. The least you can do is give them a minute to look at each other."

Robertson nodded to one of the men next to Millie and he removed the blindfold. Then Robertson led Millie's horse to the rear of the wagon where she could see Seth.

"Oh, Grandpa! Grandpa! What have they done to you?" Millie's distress echoed in her voice.

Before Ruddell could answer, Robertson handed the reins of Millie's horse to one of his minions who led Millie to the front of the wagon.

"Let's get on with this," Robertson said. "I want to get out to my new ranch before dark. Me and the boys plan to have a party."

While this business was going on, Jason Barton and his pack of jackals entered town. They strutted their horses down the street, following their black-suited leader like Napoleon's Army entering a conquered city, or Sherman's troops marching to the sea. Many were obviously drunk. Each man carried a crude torch made of rags tied to the ends of short poles. The odor of kerosene filled the air. This second gaggle of henchmen stopped twenty yards behind the first group. They would be the satanic spectators of the travesty that was about to unfold.

Because Ruddell was unable to leave the wagon, Porter found a smooth wooden plank to use as a hard surface for signing the deed and got into the back of the wagon. Robertson, told he needed to sign the document as well, climbed on board and stood next to Ruddell.

Porter dipped the pen point into an ink bottle and handed the pen to Ruddell. With a shaking hand, Ruddell moved the pen toward the deed.

"NO SIGN PAPER, SETH!" The booming voice of Swift Eagle reverberated down the street, bouncing from building to building like thunder from a storm.

The startled and confused stooges spun their horses quickly around, to be met face to face with Swift Eagle and fifty mounted Navajo braves, each pointing a rifle at the tightly grouped bunch of outlaws. Some of the thugs spun quickly to spur their horses in the other direction, only to be confronted by a second large party of Navajos. A white man led this group. Lester Hobson!

Immediately after Swift Eagle's shout, the bell of the church began to ring. With that, every door along both sides of the street flew open, and the sidewalks quickly filled with armed men. Most carried rifles. A few, including John Bundy, held shotguns. Jim Leklem, the pig farmer, stood in a menacing stance thrusting a pitchfork. Reverend Grassley stopped pulling the bell rope and stepped through the doorway of the church waving his weapon—the *Holy Bible.*

The double doors of the schoolhouse swung open wide and Lorna Porter, resplendent in dark brown leather trousers and jacket, ran quickly down the steps, followed by her two brothers.

Barton was furious, and screamed at his ragtag crew, "Kill them! Kill them all! You yellow-bellied cowards! Kill them!"

One of the riffraff, attempting to follow Barton's order,

took aim at Morgan but was knocked out of his saddle by a bullet from Swift Eagle's rifle. Another, attempting to make a run for it, was lassoed by Hobson and dragged for a short distance through the muddy street.

Surprise and confusion held sway over the band of outlaws. Realizing they were boxed on all sides—and outnumbered four to one by an outraged community—the hooligans quickly dropped their guns and torches and put their hands high in the air.

Robertson, in a split second, saw his dream of possessing the Rocking Ewe evaporate. He knew, without Barton's protection, he would have to answer for his crimes.

In a fit of wild rage, Robertson drew his revolver, pointed it at Ruddell's head, and shouted, "Now you die, old man!"

The roar of a shotgun blast split the morning air. Robertson's buckshot-filled carcass elevated three feet above the side of the wagon and slammed hard onto the wet street. Smoke drifted skyward through a large hole blown in the blanket covering Ruddell.

While attention was diverted to Robertson, Barton had a chance to make a break for it. But he chose instead to gun down Morgan, hoping for a small measure of satisfaction from this embarrassing fiasco. Barton, with both pearl-handled revolvers drawn, spurred his horse toward Morgan, thirty yards away. A maniacal scream shattered the air.

"Watch it, Clem!" Jakes shouted. "Watch it!"

Morgan, hearing and seeing the charging Barton headed

directly for him, jumped from his horse, rolled under the wagon, quick-drew his Colt and blasted Barton with two bullets to the chest, somersaulting him backward from his horse. Barton's dead body, with eyes open and staring in disbelief, had fallen crosswise on top of Robertson.

The ebony cloud of fear and uncertainty that had shrouded Red Mountain for days suddenly gave way to a shining promise of better times to come.

The good people whooped and cheered.

The bad guys pleaded for mercy.

With no place to put the defeated riffraff, Morgan and Porter decided to turn them loose—without their weapons—and send them on their way. Mayor Porter issued a stern warning they were never to be seen anywhere near Red Mountain again. If anyone was stupid enough to return, he'd be shot on sight. Swift Eagle gave the same warning from the Navajos. Morgan and Jakes reasoned that without a leader to direct their every move, these morons would go back to drifting. To make their return even more difficult, and dismantle their ability to function as a gang, the Navajos would ride with the outlaws, taking them, individually, far into the southland before turning them loose. The fat man Jakes brought in would also be escorted from the territory.

The job of getting Barton's and Robertson's bodies back to Bartonville for burial went to Hunt. Although the boy seemed truly repentant for his involvement with Robertson, and promised he would give the people of Bartonville a true accounting of all that happened, he was warned to never be seen near Red Mountain again.

Millie and Clark took Ruddell back to Porter's house to be looked after. It seemed to everyone that with Millie's return, much of Ruddell's old spirit had rekindled.

Mayor Porter invited everyone to the church. Most were eager to get home to their families, or just get out of town for a while, but a few followed him to the church. When the meeting started, a head count showed nine in attendance: Porter, Morgan, Jakes, Lorna Porter, Swift Eagle, Hobson, Bundy, Reverend Grassley and Leklem.

After the reverend delivered a brief prayer of praise and thanksgiving, the mayor opened the floor for questions and comments. Then he asked the first question.

"I'm just busting to know how so many people showed up here today. When the boys and I made the rounds looking for help, and when I came here to the church on Sunday, no one wanted to get involved. What happened?"

"I'll tell you what happened," Leklem offered. "Your daughter happened, that's what happened. She come ridin' out to our place and lit into me like I ain't ever been lit into before. She didn't yell or nothin' like that. Would've been a lot easier if she had. She just looked me in the eye and asked if I liked livin' here, and did I like my neighbors, and if I answered 'yes' to them questions, then why didn't I have enough gumption to fight for my land, and help them neighbors out?

"Well, sir, I had an answer to the livin' here part, but I couldn't come up with a reason to say where my gumption had gone. Then she told me I needed to start bein' a leader and, because I was so ornery, if I decided to fight for my land and my friends, everyone else would too. Made me feel small and big at the same time.

"So we got busy and spread the word Jim Leklem was gonna fight, and all who wanted to join should be in town after dark on Monday. Smokin' Joe, I hadn't no idea so many would come. Then Lorna took over. She parceled us out and said to get into the buildings and stay in the dark all night, then come out when the church bell rung. So that's what we did."

Morgan's smile filled with warm, loving pride of Lorna as he squeezed her hand.

"So how did Swift Eagle get involved?" Morgan asked Lorna. "Did you go from hogan to hogan looking for help?"

"No." Lorna laughed. "When the Navajos showed up this morning, I was as surprised as anyone."

Swift Eagle looked at Hobson. "You tell, Lester. You make better talk than Swift Eagle."

"First off, let me tell a little somethin'," Lester said. "Me an' Swift Eagle go way back. His pa an' my pa was scouts fer the Army when they was chasin' Mexican cattle rustlers back an' forth 'cross the border. They got ta be real good friends. They was blood brothers when they died. 'Fore they went out on that last march, my pa took me ta live with Swift Eagle's folk, 'cause my ma died that winter. Well, both our pas got kilt, an' never come back, so Swift Eagle's ma reared me like I was one a' hers.

"Swift Eagle had a sister I was sweet on, an' she was sweet on me too. Problem was, her pa done promised her ta someone else. Me an' her tried ta sneak away one night. Swift Eagle caught us an' he beat the puddin' outta me. Made me leave the village.

"I knocked 'round fer years, then hired on with Seth. When Swift Eagle come there ta work, it was hard on both a' us, but we hung in there, fer Seth. Then the darnedest thin' happened. When everbody thunk I kilt the sheriff, Swift Eagle come an' found me, where he knowed I'd be hidin', an' he took me ta his village. I been there ever since.

"Late Sunday, Swift Eagle an' his three buddies come back from the Rockin' Ewe, tellin' 'bout what them Bartonville rats was gonna do. They was riled up somethin' fierce, so them an' Swift Eagle sent out a call for men ta come an' help save Red Mountain. We got there this mornin' when it was still dark, so we split up in two bunches an' hid out 'til we knowed Millie was gonna be okay.

"We didn't 'spect we was gonna git all that help from you folks."

Shortly after the meeting adjourned, Leklem and Bundy headed for home, Swift Eagle and Hobson started back to the Navajo village, and the others went to Porter's house to check on Ruddell. Morgan and Lorna wanted to walk, so Jakes led Morgan's gelding to the house.

The two ambled down the street, hand in hand, neither wanting to speak. The day had been long, tense, and horrendous by any account. Although it was only a little after noon, both were mentally and physically fatigued. A half-block from the house, Morgan stopped walking and looked into Lorna's sparkling emerald eyes.

"I'm so proud of you, lady," he said. Then he gently kissed her dry lips.

Arriving at the house, they were surprised to see Clark and Jakes carrying Ruddell to the wagon. Millie was following close behind.

"What's happening, Ben?" Morgan asked. "You going somewhere?"

"Dang, right!" Ruddell said firmly, before Clark could answer. "I need to get home. Can't spend time layin' about here in town. I got a ranch to run."

"He's as stubborn as he ever was." Millie laughed. "He's made up his mind he's going home, so there's no need to argue with him."

"I'll give him credit for one thing. For a man at death's door a few hours ago, he sure seems to be full of his old pepper."

Jakes would ride along to the Rocking Ewe and help Clark get Ruddell into the house and in bed.

"I'll gather up my things while I'm there, Clem, and be back here in the mornin'," Jakes said. "Then I'll be headin' back to Pueblo. You comin' with me?"

"We'll see about that, Jamison. I should know by morning."

Chapter Twenty

Soon after the wagon rolled out of Red Mountain toward the Rocking Ewe, Clemet Morgan and Lorna Porter sat in the front porch swing, each deep in thought. Morgan smiled when he realized he still had the sheriff's badge pinned to his shirt. He slowly removed it, held it in the palm of his hand, and watched the afternoon rays reflect on the metal.

Amos and Elsie Porter, exhausted from the uncertainty of all that had haunted their lives for the past three days, were napping in their bedroom. The boys, at the request of their father, were cleaning the livery and the blacksmith forge. Porter had been so busy trying to hold his town together his work had piled up.

Morgan held Lorna's hand tightly in his. Each seemed to wait for the other to say something. Morgan wanted to explain to Lorna what she had come to mean to him, but feared he couldn't find the right words, that his expression of love would fall short of what he was feeling. He needed to do it right. Lorna was thinking perhaps she had already said too much, that she had been too forward in letting Morgan know of her love. So, they sat in silence—each hoping the other would have the courage to speak.

Jakes got back to Red Mountain the following morning, a little before noon, and went directly to Porter's house looking for Morgan. Jakes' saddlebags bulged with clothes and food for the trail. He was headed for home in Pueblo and eager to get on the road. Elsie Porter told him Morgan and Lorna had walked to the general store more than an hour before.

Jakes dismounted and gave Elsie a tight good-bye hug.

"God go with you, Jamison," Elsie said, a tear rolling down her cheek. "Thanks for all you did to help us. Make sure you stop by the livery to see Amos. I know he'll want to see you before you go."

"I'll sure do that, ma'am."

As Jakes neared the livery, Morgan and Lorna were coming toward him from the direction of the general store. They waved broadly to each other, and Morgan let out a loud whoop, bringing Porter from his barn.

Jakes reported all was well at the Rocking Ewe. Harry Samuels heard about the ruckus in town and already was back at work, as were Swift Eagle, Lester Hobson, and the three Navajos. They, along with Clark, were on their way to round up the sheep and get them back inside the compound. Samuels would be hiring more men after giving the old-timers first refusal rights.

Before Jakes left the Rocking Ewe, Rudell wrote a letter to the Hunts, Wanda Robertson's parents, and asked Jakes to deliver it on his way through Bartonville. The letter expressed Seth's sincere condolences to the family over their loss. Also, assuming Robertson's girls would be the heirs to the Alawanda, and the Hunts their guardians, Seth was making a generous offer to buy the ranch.

Smiling broadly at Amos Porter, Jakes said, "Looks like you'll have some official business comin' your way Mayor. Millie and Ben Clark will be tyin' the knot soon and they want you to do the honors."

Jakes paused for a minute and took a deep breath. "Well, I'm hittin' the trail for home. Most likely, I got me another mouth to feed. You comin' with me, partner?"

"Nope," Morgan said with a grin. "Seems like this is the season for weddings. Last night I asked Lorna to marry me. And all is right with the world—she said yes! We told her family this morning and when Amos didn't reach for his shotgun, I figured it was okay with them too."

"More than okay," Porter responded. "Not only do we get us one heck of a son-in-law, but Red Mountain gets a sheriff."

"Can you make it, just bein' sheriff?" Jakes asked Morgan. "Will you keep workin' for Seth too?"

"No. We just talked with Nell Gainer and she accepted

our offer to buy the general store. So, I'll do like Harold. We'll run the store full time and I'll pin on my badge when it's called for. Lorna will fill in at the school when they need help so she can spend time with the children."

"Well, congratulations, Clem! You're one lucky cuss, that's for sure. What'll we do about the office?"

"I want you have it. I'll need to get up there and withdraw my money from the bank. We'll take care of transferring the business then. Lorna and I think Pueblo will be a real nice place for a honeymoon."

"It will be, for a fact. How long will you be stayin'?"

"Just long enough for me to learn how to operate a telegraph. Red Mountain needs to get back in touch with the rest of the world."

"Me and Maryalice will be lookin' for you and Missus Morgan," Jakes said cheerfully as he vaulted into his saddle, and slowly rode away.

Then he stopped for a minute and looked back.

"Be happy and well," he said. "All of you be happy and well!"